HEREIN you will find familiar folklore elements: a young woman traveling through the Kingdoms of the Green Isles with a witch staff in her hand, a harp on her back, a puzzle to solve, a quest to fulfill. But like the very best of the old folk tales and the new fantasy novels that grow out of them, these elements are reshaped into a fresh new form by the poetic magic of a master storyteller.

In this brand-new novel by one of the most popular fantasy writers of our time, Canadian author, Celtic folklorist and musician Charles de Lint brings new life to ancient myths, following in the footsteps of such fantasy masters as J.R.R. Tolkien, C.S. Lewis, Andre Norton and Ursula K. Le Guin.

"De Lint can feel the beauty of the ancient lore he is evoking. He can well imagine what it would be like to conjure the Other World among ancient standing stones. His characters have certain fallibility that makes them multi-dimensional and human, and his settings are gritty. This is no Disneylike Never-Never Land...Life and death in de Lint's world are more than a matter of a few words or magic crystal. The Sidhe are beguiling, terrifying folk and their Otherworld a realm from which no mortal returns unchanged. De Lint knows that, regardless of what names he uses."

—*The Philadelphia Inquirer*

"For more than a decade, Charles de Lint has enjoyed a reputation as one of the world's leading fantasists."

—*The Toronto Star*

By Charles de Lint
from Tom Doherty Associates, Inc.

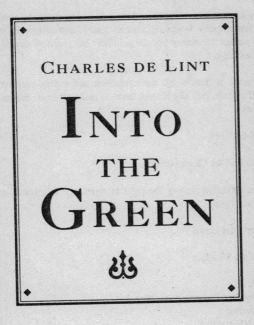

CHARLES DE LINT

INTO THE GREEN

A TOM DOHERTY ASSOCIATES BOOK
NEW YORK

This is a work of fiction. All the characters and events portrayed in this book are fictitious, and any resemblance to real people or events is purely coincidental.

INTO THE GREEN

Copyright © 1993 by Charles de Lint

Cover art by John Howe

Edited by Terri Windling

A Tor Book
Published by Tom Doherty Associates, Inc.
175 Fifth Avenue
New York, NY 10010

Tor® is a registered trademark of Tom Doherty Associates, Inc.

ISBN: 0-812-52249-4
Library of Congress Catalog Card Number: 93-2654

First edition: November 1993
First mass market edition: January 1995

Printed in the United States of America

0 9 8 7 6 5 4 3 2 1

for the Oxford boys & girls
(official and honorary)
for songs, support
and great good cheer

With special thanks to MZB,
who first sent me looking for these stories,
and to Diana for her own.

AUTHOR'S NOTE

The early portion of this novel appeared, in much altered form, as short stories in Marion Zimmer Bradley's SWORD AND SORCERESS anthology series from DAW Books.

To those interested in this kind of thing, "Angharad" is pronounced "Ann-ar-ad," "ar" pronounced as it is in "car," "ad," as in "lad".

Heather am I and I restore luck
I am the queen of every hive
Reddening the mountains in midsummer
Stag and stone revere my harping

—Wendelessen,
from "Four Seasons,
and the First Day of the Year"

the Kingdoms of the Green Isles
Dathen ~ Gwendellan ~ Ardmeyn
Ardmeyn
the Thornbrow Mountains
Taynvell Peak
the East Marches
Langstone
Goks Isles
Becks Bay
the Inverisles
the West Marches
the Narrows
Were Wood
Twellen
Wickenfirue
Pelamas Henge
Erlwen Stone
Ramshorn Mts.
Waysdown
Kellmidden
Crinan
Saewell
Dales of Heatherby
Calpstone
Lindesweir
Dergwyth Wood
Traws
Kynan
Umbria
Pishuan
Carawyn Hills
Berwin Mts.
Poole
Lethaven
Fletten
The High Walk
Keddlehowe
Yellfennie
Cermyn
Wennys Hollow
Swaston
Windbourne
West Meon Mts.
Ball Stone
Avalarn
Godswill
Ippswillow
Flooden
Nowe
Hemembraw Wood
Mullyn
Glenstone
Hayling Peaks
Tallifold
Wen-Stone
Stairn
Mull Isles
Isle of Morennen
Harl's Bay
Horn Henge
Lenhart
Tiercaern
Channel Sea
North Gwendellan
Wickster
Jevan
Gnarlwood
Ammer Peaks
Reedstone
Abercarn
Eynshorn
Billesdown
Titch Peaks
Rollestone
Samberton
South Gwendellan
Meirion
Ullan
Cathal
Weaver Henge
Ancroft
Forhold
Grey Sea
Mewer
Taw Isle
Cumstone
Addlesten Peaks
Fairnland
Shrewstone
Kettering
Owshenge
Mullion
Dathen Isle
N
E
S
W
0 25 50 75 100
Miles

INTO THE GREEN

I

ANGHARAD'S PEOPLE MET the witches the night they camped by Tiercaern, where the heather-backed Carawyn Hills flow down to the sea.

There were two of them—an old winter of a man, with salt-white hair and skin as brown and wrinkled as a tinker's hand, and a boy Angharad's age, fifteen summers if he was a day, lean and whip-thin, with hair as black as a sloe. They had the flicker of blue-gold in the depths of their eyes—eyes that were both old and young, of all ages and of none.

The tinkers had brought their canvas-topped wagons around in a circle and were preparing supper when the pair approached the edge of the camp. They hailed the tinkers above the sudden warning chorus of the camp dogs, and Angharad's father, Herend'n, went out to meet them, for he was the leader of the company.

"Is there iron on you?" Herend'n called, by which he meant, were they carrying weapons.

The old man shook his head and lifted his staff. It was a white wood, that staff; cut from a rowan: witch-wood.

"Not unless you count this," he said. "My name's Woodfrost and this is Garrow, my grandson. We are travelers—like yourselves."

Angharad, peering at the strangers from behind her father's back, saw the blue-gold light in their eyes and shook her head. They weren't like her people. They weren't at all like any tinkers *she* knew.

Her father regarded the strangers steadily for a long heartbeat, then stepped aside and ushered them into the wagon circle.

"Be welcome," he said.

When they were by his fire, he offered them the guest-cup with his own hands. Woodfrost took the tea and sipped. Seeing them up close, Angharad wondered why the housey-folk feared witches so. This pair was as bedraggled as a couple of cats caught out in a storm and seemed no more frightening to her than beggars in a market town square. They were skinny and poor, with ragged travel-stained cloaks and unkempt hair. But then the old man's gaze touched hers and suddenly Angharad *was* afraid.

There was a distance in those witch-eyes, like a night sky rich with stars, or like a hawk floating high on the wind, watching, waiting to drop on its prey. They read something in her, pierced the scurry of her thoughts and the motley mix of what she was, to find something lacking. She couldn't look away, she was trapped like a riddle on a raven's tongue, until he finally dropped his gaze. Shivering, Angharad moved closer to her father.

"I thank you for your kindness," Woodfrost said as he handed the guest-cup back to Herend'n. "The road can be hard for folk such as we—especially when there is no home waiting for us at road's end."

Again his gaze touched Angharad.

"Is this your daughter?" he added.

Herend'n nodded proudly and gave the old man her name. He was a widower and with the death of Angharad's mother many years ago much of his joy in life had died. But if he loved anything in this world, it was his colt-thin daughter with her brown eyes that were so big and the bird's-nest tangle of her red hair.

"She has the sight," Woodfrost said.

"I know," Herend'n replied. "Her mother had it too—Ballan rest her soul."

Bewildered, Angharad looked from her father to the stranger. This was the first *she'd* heard of it.

"But Da," she said, pulling at his sleeve.

He turned at the tug to look at her. Something passed across his features the way the grass in a field trembles like a wave when the wind touches it. It was there one moment, gone the next—a sadness, a touch of pride, a momentary fear.

"But, Da," she repeated.

"Don't be afraid," he said. "It's but a gift—like Kinny's skill with a fiddle, or the way Sheera can set a snare and talk to her ferrets."

"I'm not a witch!"

"It isn't such a terrible thing," Woodfrost said gently.

Angharad refused to meet his gaze. Instead, she looked at the boy. He smiled back shyly. Quickly Angharad looked away.

"I'm not," she said again, but now she wasn't so sure.

She wasn't exactly sure what the sight was, but she could remember a time when she'd seen more in the world than those around her. But she'd been so young then and it all went away when she grew up.

Or she had made it go away . . .

As though the coming of the witches was a catalyst, Angharad found that once again she could see what was hidden from others. Again she was aware of movement abroad in the world that went unseen and unheard by both tinkers and the housey-folk who lived in the towns or worked the farms, and to see it, to hear it, was not such a terrible thing.

Woodfrost and Garrow traveled with the company that whole summer long and will she, nill she, Angharad learned to use her gift. She retained her fear of Woodfrost—because there was always that shadow, that darkness, that secrecy in his eyes—but she made friends with Garrow. He was still shy with the other tinkers, but he opened up to her. His secrets, when they unfolded, were of a far and distant sort from what she supposed his grandsire's to be.

Garrow taught her the language of the trees and the beasts, from the murmur of a drowsy oak to the quick chatter of squirrel and finch, and the sly tongue of the fox. Magpies became her confidants, and badgers, and the wind. But at the same time she found herself becoming tongue-tied around Garrow. If he paid particular attention to her, or caught one of her long dreamy glances, a flush would rise from the nape of her neck and her heart began to beat quick and fast like that of a captured wren.

On a night between the last days of the Summerlord Hafarl's rule and the first cold days of autumn, on a night when the housey-folk left their farms and towns to build great bonfires on the hilltops where they sang and danced to music that made the priests of the One God Dath frown, she and Garrow made a mystery of their own. They made love as gently fierce as the stag and moon in the spring and, afterwards, lay dreamy and content in each other's arms while the stars completed their nightly wheel and spin in the skies high above them.

When Garrow finally slept, tears touched Angharad's cheeks, but it wasn't for sorrow that she wept. She was so full of emotion and magic that there was simply no other release for what she felt swelling inside her.

The tinker company wintered in Mullion that year, on a farm that belonged to Green George Snell, who once traveled the roads with Angharad's people. There they prepared for the next year's traveling. Wagons were repaired, as were harnesses and riggings. Goods were made to be sold at the market towns and the horses were readied for the fairs.

When the first breath of spring was in the air, the company took to the road once more. Angharad and Garrow still rode in Herend'n's wagon, though they had jumped the broom at midwinter. Newly married, they were still too poor to afford their own wagon.

The road took them up into Umbria and Kellmidden that summer, where the company looked to meet with the caravans of other travelers and to grow rich—or at least as rich as any tinker could get, which was not a great deal by the standards of the housey-folk. They looked forward to a summer of traveling and the road, of gossiping and trading, of renewing old acquaintances and making new friends.

Instead, they found the plague waiting for them.

2

THE SIGHT OF that first devastated town cut into Angharad like a sharp sliver thrust deep into her heart. All she could do was stare at the corpse where it lay in the town square, black and swollen. Around her, the tinkers' shocked gazes found more bodies, and then more still—in alleyways, in doorways. The entire population of the town was an ungainly sprawl of corpses, black from the plague, lying wherever they'd fallen and taken their last breath.

Too late, Herend'n realized their plight.

The town had been oddly silent, but the tinkers hadn't remarked on that as their wagons rolled out of the moors and made their way down the long gentle slope to where the buildings clustered by the river ford. Not one of them had noticed the lack of smoke rising from the chimneys of the buildings, the empty streets, the disquiet of the camp dogs, the empty pastures about the town.

It wasn't until they reached the town square, where that first corpse lay blocking their way, that they realized something was dangerously amiss, and by then it was too late.

Herend'n allowed no one to alight. He immediately

turned the wagons and prayed to the Lord of Broom and Heather to protect them; but two nights later the first of the company took sick all the same. In retrospect, Herend'n realized that one of the camp dogs must have spread the sickness. When Angharad and the witches *saw* the plague spreading under the skin of Marenda's son Fearnol, Herend'n turned the wagons into their circle and they set up camp.

But it was far too late.

By nightfall, half the company was stricken. In two weeks' time, for all the medicines that Angharad and the witches and the rootwives of the tinkers gathered and prepared and fed to the sick, the greater part of the company was dead.

Nine wagons were in that circle and sixty-two tinkers had traveled in them. On the morning that the last of the dead were buried, only one wagon left the camp and only three of the company rode in it. They were thin and gaunt as half-starved ravens: Jend'n the Tall, Sheera's daughter Benraida, and Crowen the Kettle-maker.

There was a fourth survivor—Angharad. But she remained behind with her dead. Her father. Her husband. Her kin. Her friends.

She lived in her father's wagon and tended their graves the whole summer long. She cursed the sight that had made her see the black sickness speed and swell inside the bodies of the stricken, killing them cell by cell, while she stood helplessly by.

Garrow. Her father . . .

She cursed what gods she knew of, from Ballan, the Lord of Broom and Heather, to Dath, the cold One God, and Hafarl's daughter to whom she had always felt the closest: gentle Tarasen, who kept safe the beasts of the wood and the birds of the air. Even she had failed Angharad in her time of need.

Angharad stayed there until the summer drew to an

end, and then she remembered a tale once heard around the fires of a tinker camp, of marshes and Jacky Lantern's kowrie kin, of how the dead could be called back in such a place, if one's need were great enough, if one had the gift . . .

She took to the road the next morning with a small pack of provisions slung over one shoulder and Woodfrost's white staff in her hand. She went through a land empty and deserted, through villages and towns where the dead lay unburied, past farms that were silent and forsaken as broken dreams. She traveled through the wild north highlands of Umbria, and when she crossed Kellmidden's borders it was to come to a land that the plague had never grasped in its diseased claws.

And still she did not understand why she had been spared when so many had died.

Hafarl's grip was loosing on the land as the autumn grew crisp across the dales and hills of Kellmidden's lowlands; the constellations that wheeled above her by night were those of Lithun, the Winterlord. She stopped to sup in a last inn, ignoring the warnings of the well-meaning housey-folk that stayed warm by the fire when she went out into the night once more.

Don't go by night, they said. But she did.

Don't stray from the road, they said. But she did.

Don't follow the fire; don't listen to its music. But she did.

They meant well, she knew, but they didn't understand. She sought the blue-gold fire and the fey music of Jacky Lantern's elusive kin.

It was all she had left.

She went empty-handed now, her provision bag depleted and the rowan staff no longer needed, for she knew she was approaching the end of her journey. As she had eaten her supper in the inn, she'd heard the sweet fey music . . . calling to her, whispering, drawing her on, unattainable as fool's fire, but calling to her all the same. When she left the road and entered the dark forests, Garrow's features swam in her mind's eye, a familiar smile playing on his lips, keyed to the fey, unearthly music that came to her from the depths of the forest.

It was then that she knew her journey was done.

3

As SHE LEFT the road, the forest closed in around her, dark and rich with scent and sound. The wind spoke in the uppermost branches with a murmur that almost, but not quite, buried the sound of a distant harp music coming to her from deeper in the wood. Her witch-sight pierced the gloom, searching for the first trace of a will-o'-the-wisp's lantern, bobbing in amongst the trees.

But there was nothing to see. There was only the music.

She hurried on, going more and more quickly. Tears ran down her cheeks as all her losses rose to follow her ever more deeply into the forest. Finally she stumbled, foot snagged by a root. She only just caught herself from falling by catching hold of a low-hanging branch. She leaned against the fat bole of the tree to which it was attached. The bark was rough against her skin and pulled at her hair as she moved her head slowly away from it.

As though echoing her pain, the distant harping faltered and grew still.

She lifted her head, afraid of the sudden silence. Then faintly, faintly, the music started up once more and she went on, trying to keep the memories buried, but they rose, constant as air bubbles in a sulfur spring, the pain spreading through her as pervasively as those noxious fumes fouled the air about themselves.

The land sloped steadily downward in the direction she was traveling. The forest of pine, birch and fir gave way to gnarly cedars and stands of willow. Underfoot, the ground softened and her passage was marked by the soft sucking noise of her feet lifting from the marshy footing.

A sliver of a horned moon was lowering in the west: Anann's last quarter, a moon of omens.

The muck rose to her ankles and the long days of her journeying and sorrow finally took their toll. Weary beyond belief, she collapsed on a small hillock that rose out of the marsh. The fey harping was no louder than it had ever been, but somehow it seemed closer now. On arms trembling from fatigue, she lifted her upper body from the ground and rolled over to see the makers of that music standing all around her.

They were tall ghostly beings, thin as reeds and glowing with their own pale inner light. Their hair hung thin and feather soft about their long and narrow faces. The men carried lanterns filled with flickering light—fool's fire; the women played harps that were as slender as willow boughs, with strings like spun moonlight. Their eyes gleamed blue-gold in the darkness.

Strayed, the harping sang to her. A ghostly refrain. *Too far . . . too far . . .*

She looked amongst their ranks for another slender form—a familiar form, with black hair and no harping skill—but saw only the ghostly harpers and lantern-bearers.

"Garrow?" she called, searching their faces.

The harping fluttered like a chorus of bird calls, then grew still. Angharad's heartbeat stilled with it. She held her breath as one of the pale glowing shapes moved forward.

"You!" she cried.

The anger in her voice was plain as she recognized the man's features. Her pulse drummed suddenly, loud in her ears, driven by a mingling of that anger and fear.

Woodfrost nodded wearily. "You are still so stubborn," he said.

She glared at him. "What have you done with Garrow?" she demanded. "I didn't come for you, old man."

"As a child you could see," Woodfrost went on as though he hadn't heard her, "but you realized soon enough that others couldn't and, rather than be different, you ignored the gift until you became as blind as they were. Ignored it so that, in time, all memory of it was gone."

"It was a curse, not a gift," Angharad said. "How can you call it a gift when it allows you to *see* those you love die, while you must stand helplessly by?"

"So many years you wasted," Woodfrost continued, still ignoring her. "So stubborn. And then we came to your camp, my grandson and I. Still you protested, until Garrow drew the veil from your eyes and taught you your gift once more—taught you what you had once known, but chose to forget. Was your gift so evil then?"

Angharad wanted to stand, but her body was too tired to obey her. She managed to sit up and hug her knees.

"Garrow was alive then," she said.

Woodfrost nodded. "So he was. And then he died. Death is a tragedy—no mistake of that, Angharad—but only for the living. We who have died go on to . . . other things, as the living must go on with the responsibility of being alive. But not you. Oh, no. You are too stubborn for that. If those you love are dead, then you will go about as one dead yourself. It is a fine thing to revere those who have passed on—but only within reason, Angharad. Graves may be tended and memories called up, but the business of living must go on."

"I could call him back," Angharad said in a small voice. "In this place . . . I could call him back."

"Only if I let you."

Anger flickered in Angharad's witchy eyes. "You have no right to come between us."

"Angharad," Woodfrost said softly. "Do you truly believe that I would stand between you and my grandson if he were alive? When you joined your futures together, none was happier than I. But we no longer speak of you and Garrow; we speak now of the living and the dead, and yes, I will come between you then."

"Why is it so evil to call him back? We *loved* each other."

"It is not so much evil as . . ." He sighed. "Let us leave the talk of evil and sins to the priests of Dath. Say rather that it is wrong, Angharad. You have a duty and responsibility while you live that does not include calling forth the shades of the dead. Death will come for you soon enough, for even the lives of witches are not so long as men would believe, and then you will be with Garrow in the Land of Shadows. Will you make a Land of Shadows in the world of the living?"

"Without him there is nothing."

"There is everything still."

"If you weren't already dead," Angharad said dully, "I would kill you."

"Why? Because I speak the truth? You are a woman of the traveling people—not some village-bound goodwife who looks to her husband for every approval."

"It's not that. It's . . ."

Her voice trailed off. She stared past him to where the will-o'-the-wisps stood pale and tall, silent harps held in glowing hands, witchy lanterns gleaming eerily.

"I could live ten years without him," she said softly, her gaze returning to the old man's. "I could live forever without him—so long as I knew that he was still in the world. That all he was was not gone from it. That somewhere his voice was still heard, his face seen, his kindness known. Not dead. Not lying in a grave with the cold earth on him and the worms feeding on his body.

"If I could know that he was still . . . happy . . ."

"Angharad, he can be content—which is as close as the dead can come to what the living call 'happiness.' When he knows that you will go on with your life, that you will take up the reins of your witch's duties once more—then he will be at peace."

"Broom and Heather!" Angharad cried. "What duty? I have no duty. Only loss."

Woodfrost stepped towards her and lifted her to her feet. His touch was cold and eerie on her skin and she shrank back from him, but he did not let her go.

"While you live," he said, "you have a duty to life. And Hafarl's gift—the gift of the Summerblood that gives you your sight—you have a duty to it as well. The fey wonders of the world only exist while there are those with the sight to see them, Angharad. Otherwise they fade away."

"I see only a world made grey with grief."

"I have known grief as well," Woodfrost said. "I lost my wife. My daughter. Her husband. I, too, have lost loved ones, but that did not keep me from my duties to life and the gift. I traveled the roads and sought blind folk such as you were and did my best to make them see once more. Not for myself. But that the world might not lose its wonder. Its magic."

"But . . ."

The old man stepped back from her. In his gaze she saw once more that weighing look that had come into his eyes on that first night she had met him.

"If not for yourself," he said, "then do it for the others who are still blind to their gift. Is your grief so great that they must suffer for it as well?"

Angharad shrank back, more frightened by the quiet sympathy in his eyes, than if he'd been angry with her.

"I . . . I'm just one person . . ."

"So are all who live . . . and so are all who have the gift. The music of the Middle Kingdom is only a whisper now, Angharad. When it is forgotten, not even an echo of that music will remain. If you would leave such a world for those who are yet to be born, then call your husband back from the Land of Shadows and live together in some half-life—neither living nor dead, the both of you.

"The choice is yours, Angharad."

She bowed her head, tears spilling down her cheeks.

I'm not as strong as you, she wanted to tell him, but when she lifted her anguished gaze, he was no longer there. She saw only the wraith-shapes of Jacky Lantern's kin, watching her. In their faces there were no answers, no judgments. Their blue-gold eyes returned her gaze without reply.

"Garrow," she said softly, all her love caught up in that one word, that one name.

There was a motion in the air where Woodfrost had stood, a sense of some gate opening between this world and the next. Through her teary gaze she saw a familiar face taking shape, the hazy outline of a body underneath it.

"Garrow," she said again.

The image grew firmer, more substantial. For a long moment she watched him forming there, drawing substance from the marsh, breaching the gulf between the Land of Shadows and the hillock where she stood. Then she bowed her head once more.

"Go gentle," she said.

She could feel his presence vanish without the need to watch. Her throat was thick with emotion, her eyes blinded by tears. Then there was a touch on her cheek, like lips of wind brushing against her skin, here one moment like a feather, then gone. He was lost now, lost forever, while she must go on. In the midst of her grief, a strange warmth rose up in her, and she thought she heard a voice, distant, distant, whispering.

I will wait for you, my love . . .

And then she was alone in the marsh, with only the ghostly will-o'-the-wisps for company.

Through a sheen of tears, she watched one of the harpers approach her, the woman's pale shape more gossamer than ever. She laid her harp on Angharad's knee. Like Woodfrost's hands, it had substance and weight, surprising her—but there was no eerie chill in its wood. It was a small plain instrument—more like a child's harp than those that the itinerant barden carried and played. She touched the smooth wood of its curving neck.

"I . . . I'm a witch," she said in a low soft voice, the bitterness in it directed only at herself. "I can't make music—I never could."

But her fingers were drawn to the strings and she found that they knew a melody, if she did not. It was a slow sad air that drew the sorrow from her and made of it a haunting music that eased the pain inside her.

A kowrie gift, she thought. Was it supposed to make her grief more bearable?

"It must have a name," the wraith said, her voice uncanny and echoing like the breath of a wind on a far hill.

A name? Angharad thought.

She watched her fingers draw the music from the instrument's strings and wondered that wood and metal could make such a sound.

A name?

Her sadness was in the harp's music, loosened from

the tight knots inside her and set free on the air where the night healed it.

"I will call it Garrow," she said, looking up.

The ghostly company was gone, but she no longer felt so alone.

4

AUTUMN TURNED COLD. The frosts came and then the snows, and Angharad wintered with a shepherd and his wife in their croft, nestled in the highlands of Kellmidden near Crinan. Through the short days and long nights of that winter, she made herself useful with the carding of wool and weaving, but still found time to explore the music she discovered gathering in her thoughts, a music that was so easily pulled from the strings of the small harp with which the kowrie had gifted her.

It was that music and her ability to call it forth—she who, before that night in the fens, could scarcely hold a tune—that gave her a purpose when she set out again on the roads come spring. The ghosts and kowrie might all have been a dream, and sometimes it was easy to think of them as such, but she had but to pick up the harp to know the truth.

There was witchery and magic afoot in the world still; it wasn't merely the stuff of legends, but it *was* fading. What she had learned was that it need not disappear entirely, not when those with Hafarl's witchy blood still lived in the Green Isles. So as Woodfrost had done before her, she took to the tinker roads to find those with the Summerblood sleeping in their veins, and finding them, she woke Hafarl's gift in them so that they could add to the wonder of the world, rather than hide from it, or add to its decline.

Spring was still fresh on the land when she walked out of Kellmidden's highlands and met with a tinker company camped by a stream with good pasture nearby. She was still a young, red-haired tinker woman when she came to their wagons, but her eyes were old now, and she carried a small harp slung from her shoulder as well as a witch's rowan staff.

The tinkers welcomed her readily with a guest-cup and a place by the fire when she called out to them in their own secret tongue. Sitting in the flickering light cast by their fires, Angharad looked from face to face as she was introduced to the various families that made up the company, smiling as her gaze finally rested on a lanky girl named Zia who by Angharad's reckoning was thirteen summers old, give or take a season.

Zia blushed and looked away, but Angharad knew that inside her breast the young tinker girl felt something stir that had been buried when she learned the ways of a woman and set aside her favorite doll with its cloth face and broom and heather body.

Smiling again, Angharad began to play her harp.

But while spring came to the Green Isles, there was a place across the Grey Sea to which such seasonal changes were unknown. The Great Kharanan Desert knew only two seasons: hot and hotter. It lay far to the east on the mainland, a vast wasteland that encompassed thousands of square miles of unrelieved sand and stone. There were waterholes and oases, but they lay few and far between and were known only to the nomadic Kharanan tribes that inhabited the wasteland. Those who dared its reaches were either tribesmen or fools.

Behan g'n Khohr was not a fool. He stood at the crest of a wave of sand in that part of the Kharanan that his people called the Unforgiving Sea of Sands and shaded his eyes. What he saw in the trough below the dune on which he stood made his normally stern features slacken in surprise.

Beyond the boundaries of the Kharanan, legend had it that once the whole of the desert was a kingdom of graceful cities, gentle pastures and woodlands. But the inhabitants of that land had raised the ire of their god and in his wrath he had brought the sands to cover their kingdom and erase all memory of their presence.

The tribesmen had no such legends; the ancient kingdom with its cities and richly watered lands was a part of their history. They remembered, the tale passed on from one generation to another by their singers and shamanic *caliyeh*. They remembered, and lived their lives by the strict tenets of their faith so that one day, as promised, Jaromund, holy be His name, would take back His sands and return Kharanan to its former glory.

So when Behan saw the temple spire growing from the sand below, he fell to his knees and bowed in thanks, touching his brow to the sand. The trailing edges of his headcloth, held in place by a decorative fillet of thick woolen cords wound round with gold, silver and silk thread and ornamented with tufts of goat hair, fell to either side of his face.

"My unworthy life be His," he murmured.

Still bowing, he lifted the end of the tassled cord that lay against the breast of his robes and kissed the knot there.

"Jaromund, holy be His name, I thank you for this gift."

His heart sang with the news he would bring back to

the camp. The sands were receding. Jaromund, holy be His name, had finally forgiven His unworthy followers. Once again the Kharanan would blossom so that where now was sand would all be oasis.

He remained in a position of obeisance for a long time. The sun rose first one finger, then three, in the sky above him as he prayed, his right hand clenched tightly around his prayer knot. He murmured the ten-and-thirty blessings, followed by the twelve chants of repentance. Then finally he sat back on his haunches to study the spire below him.

It rose some seven feet from the encroaching sand, revealing, from his vantage point, the intricately detailed stone work that rose to its fluted tip and one paned window. It was a miracle, he thought, that the sands had not crushed that window.

An hour passed, then another, as he sat in contemplation of the marvelous sight. But slowly a change came over him. The joy faded in his heart as he watched the sands, not recede, but rise against the stonework.

We are still unworthy, he realized. Jaromund, holy be His name, was still displeased with His people.

With that realization, the holiness of the moment fled. He rose to his feet and stretched his cramped leg muscles. Hefting his pack, he began his descent to the spire. The sands rose to mid-calf as he went down the side of the dune, threatening to fill his red goatskin boots, and the footing was unsteady, but he reached the window without mishap. He tapped a knuckle against the glass, hand lifting to his prayer knot as a hollow echo returned.

Taking the curved knife from his belt, he wedged it between the window and its frame, working along the edge until he caught the inside clasp against the tip of his blade. A quick flip of his wrist popped the clasp. The window pried easily open and a wave of cool stale air came from inside, brushing against his face like the passage of a ghost.

Behan frowned, considering. His eyes, the startling blue of a southern tribesman, appeared paler than ever against the dark cast of his skin.

If this were a holy site, he thought, might not Jaromund, holy be His name, be displeased with its breaching?

Ah yes, his curiosity argued back. But would Jaromund, holy be His name, have allowed the sand to uncover the spire, did He not wish Behan to explore its interior?

Curiosity won. He took a torch from his pack and unwrapped the leather that covered the oil-soaked cloths wrapped about one end. Coaxing a flame from the clay ember-jar that hung from his pack, he lit the torch and thrust it in ahead of his head and shoulders as he leaned over the ledge to look inside. The torch's flickering light showed an empty chamber, heavy with dust. The window was at chest height from the stone floor. At the far side of the room was the head of a staircase.

Behan dropped his pack in first, then followed it inside. He stood for a moment on the dusty floor, looking outside at the sand dunes, judging the wind. There was time. It would be many hours before the sands rose high enough to block his retreat. So assured, he left his pack by the window and went exploring.

The staircase wound down to the next floor in a circular fashion, revealing another empty chamber. Behan continued to follow the winding stairs until he had counted seven stories. He marveled at the height this structure had once commanded, then marveled still more when he considered how the sands had covered it all.

It was on what would have been the ground floor that he came across the first piece of furnishing. Set in the middle of the chamber was what appeared to be a stone altar that, on closer inspection, proved to have a movable lid. Wedging his torch in a wall sconce near the base of the stairs, he strained at the stone lid of the altar, finally shifting it enough that he could peer within.

A small square shape lay inside, wrapped in silk and bound with a filigreed rope of braided goat's hair. When Behan had unwrapped the silk covering, he found himself holding an ebony puzzle-box, inlaid with silver designs that made him feel slightly queasy as he followed their pattern. He turned it over and over in his hands, then finally wrapped it once more and set it on the lid of the altar.

He turned his attention to the two doors on either side of the chamber, but neither would open. The desert lay behind them, he realized—the millions of tons of sand of the Unforgiving Sea of Sands that had swallowed the structure.

The thought of the weight of all that sand pressing against the walls of the tower made him suddenly uneasy.

He returned to the altar and picked up the puzzle-box. Retrieving his torch from the sconce he hurried back up all the winding twists of the stairway, breathing a sigh of relief when he found the square of window still uncovered on the top floor. He thrust the box into his pack and tossed it out the window, quickly following it himself.

He paused there a moment after he had put out his torch. He wrapped the oil-soaked cloth with leather once more and returned the torch to his pack, all the while studying that window. Finally he closed it once more and retreated up the steep incline of the dune. The sands, he noted, had risen a good foot and a half in the short while he'd been inside. By this time tomorrow, the window would be covered again. Another day, and the spire itself would be swallowed by the sands once more.

It was likely that he was the first man in a thousand years to see that structure. And he might be the last for another thousand years. But the next to come would find it even emptier than he had, for now not even the puzzle-box lay hidden away in its secret depths.

An odd find, he thought, remembering the queasy feeling that had stolen over him as he had followed the silver patterning inlaid in the wood. Perhaps Yeuhanin would know what to make of it.

Swinging his pack onto his back, he set off once more, continuing his interrupted journey back to camp.

The tent of Yeuhanin g'n Khohr stood slightly apart from those of the rest of the camp, the natural color of its goat-skins a stark contrast to the brightly painted tents of the other tribesmen. Yeuhanin was the tribesmen's *caliyeh*—part priest, part shaman; their link to Jaromund, holy be His name. Unlike the other men of the tribe, he wore loose baggy trousers and a short caftan against which hung his prayer knots—thirteen in all. His feet were bare, a white turban hid his long grey hair, and his pale eyes were surrounded with a webwork of ochre tattoos that also covered his right brow and his left cheek.

Behan went directly to Yeuhanin's tent when he reached the camp, not even stopping to see his wives and children. The puzzle-box played on his mind, making him increasingly uneasy; its patterns wouldn't leave his thoughts. Outside the door flap of the *caliyeh*'s tent, he coughed once, then waited.

"Enter," Yeuhanin said after a moment's pause.

The interior of the tent was lit with the dim glow of oil lamps that also filled the air with a perfumed scent. The *caliyeh* sat cross-legged by his small cast-iron brazier. A half-completed prayer weaving lay across his knees. On the brazier, a teapot sent a thin tendril of steam up to the roof of the tent.

Behan laid his pack by the door and approached the brazier. He lifted his prayer knot and kissed it before seating himself across from the *caliyeh*.

"I am most sorry to disturb you, Caliyeh Yeuhanin," he said with his head bowed.

The *caliyeh* nodded, accepting Behan's respectful greeting.

"Tell me your troubles," he said.

His voice was gentle, but his eyes burned like a desert hawk's. The fire in them seemed to grow as Behan spun out his tale and then showed Yeuhanin the puzzle-box he had taken away from the tower.

"This is an evil thing," Yeuhanin said when the telling was done.

Behan nodded, apprehending the *caliyeh*'s unspoken rebuke.

"Is . . . is it an artifact of the Dead God's?" he asked in a hushed voice.

The Dead God was the antithesis of Jaromund, holy be His name. Once they were brothers, but the Dead God perverted the beauty of what Jaromund, holy be His name, had created, teaching beasts to feed upon one another and men to harbor evil in their hearts. In His anger, Jaromund, holy be His name, had called forth a hero from the tribesmen to slay His brother, but even from beyond the veils of death, the Dead God whispered to the creations of Jaromund, holy be His name, urging them to turn from His blessed teachings.

Deep in the Kharanan, there had been small sects who followed the tenets of the Dead God. As the years passed, their influence was no longer felt in the Great Desert itself, for they had turned their attentions to the lands beyond the boundaries of the Kharanan, where the small sects had long since grown into a religion that overshadowed all others.

Yeuhanin gazed at the puzzle-box, a troubled look in his pale eyes. Slowly he wrapped it in its silk covering once more and tied off the braided goat's-hair rope.

"Its source is a mystery that I do not care to study," he said. His gaze rose from the covered puzzle-box to lock on Behan's eyes. "You must return it to the tower in which you found it."

Behan nodded, then swallowed thickly. He thought of the sands, rising steadily to the lip of the window.

"And . . . and if the sands have reclaimed the tower?" he asked.

"Then you must send it out into the world—far from the Kharanan, far from our people."

Behan thought of the traders with whom he dealt in the towns that bordered the desert. He liked some of them, for all their heathen beliefs.

"Forgive me, Caliyeh Yeuhanin," he said, "but will it be dangerous for them—for those who live beyond the sands?"

Yeuhanin shrugged. "This," he said, touching the silk covering with a brown finger, "feeds on witches and their like. The world can be well rid of their kind."

He regarded Behan steadily for a moment, before adding, "It also works an influence on those untainted with witchery. They will not be physically hurt, but like the whispering of the Dead God, that influence will prey upon their minds, stealing their sanity. Let those who do not follow the teachings of Jaromund, holy be His name, deal with the peril should you be unable to return this thing to its tower." A grim look touched his eyes. "Their souls are already forfeit."

Behan nodded. He lifted his prayer knot and kissed it, then accepting the puzzle-box back from Yeuhanin, he made a quick retreat from the *caliyeh's* tent.

In his own tent, he ignored his wives and children. Emptying his pack of its trade goods, he added a few more provisions and refilled his watersack from the large clay water jar by the door flap, then set out immediately for the tower, for all that he was already weary to the bone. The morning might be too late. The tower might already be gone by then.

He reached the spot where he had discovered it near midnight. A full moon sailed above the Unforgiving Sea of Sands, its bright light shimmering on the dunes. Behan stared down the trough between the dunes where the tower had stood earlier that day.

It was gone.

He gazed along his backtrail to where, hidden by distance, the camp of his people lay. On his back, the puzzle-box made such a weight of his pack that it was as though he marched with a full load.

Sighing, he turned from the road home, and began to walk along the crest of the dune towards the trading town of Sauwait.

5

ANGHARAD FOUND HIM in Avalarn, one of Cermyn's old forests, the one said long ago to have been a haunt of the wizard Puretongue. He lay in a nest of leaves, sheltered in a cleft of rocks. Above them, old oaks clawed skyward with greedy boughs, reaching for the clouds.

"I know you," he said, dark eyes opening suddenly, glittering like a crow's.

"Do you now?" she said mildly.

He was a reed-thin feral child, and she felt an immediate kinship with him. He had her red hair, and the same look of age in his eyes that she had in hers. He could have been her brother. But she had never seen him before.

"You lived in an oak," he said.

This was just another way of saying that she had a witch's sight. She rocked back on her heels as the boy sat up, and she continued to study him curiously. This was her second summer on the road, her second summer of searching out the Summerborn, and she was growing used to odd encounters.

"Are you hungry?" she asked.

When he nodded, she drew bread and cheese from

her pack and watched him devour it like a cat. He took quick bites, his gaze never leaving her face.

"I lived up in the branches of your tree once," he said, wiping crumbs from his mouth with the back of his hand. "I'd hear you playing that harp, when the moon was right."

Angharad smiled. "You heard the wind fingering an oak tree's branches—nothing else."

The boy smiled back. "So you *were* there, or how would you know? Besides, how else would a treewife play the harp of her boughs?"

His voice was soft, with a slight rasp. There was a flicker in his eyes like fool's fire.

"What's your name, boy?" she asked. "What are you doing here? Are you lost?"

"My name's Fenn and I've been waiting for you. All my life, I've been waiting for you."

Angharad couldn't help smiling again. "And such a long life you've had so far."

The boy's eyes hooded. A fox watched her from under his bushy eyebrows.

"Why have you been waiting for me?" she asked finally.

Fenn pointed to her harp. "I want you to sing the song that will set me free."

Angharad crawled through the weeds with the boy, keeping low, though out of whose sight, Fenn wouldn't say. The foothills of the West Meon Mountains ran off to the west, a sea of bell heather and gorse, dotted with islands of stone outcrops where ferrets prowled at night. But it wasn't the moorland that he'd brought her to see.

"That's where he lived," Fen said, pointing to the giant oak that stood alone and towering in the halfland between the forest and the sea of moor.

"The wizard?"

Fenn nodded. "He's bound there yet—bound to his tree. Just like you were, treewife."

"My name is Angharad," she said, not for the first time. "And I was never bound to a tree."

Fenn merely shrugged. Angharad caught his gaze and held it until he looked away, a quick sidling movement. She turned her attention back to the tree. Faintly, amongst its branches, she could make out a structure.

"That was Puretongue's tree?" she asked.

Fenn grinned, all the humor riding in his eyes. "But he's been dead a hundred years or better, of course. It's the other wizard that's bound in there now. The one that came after Puretongue."

"And what was his name?"

"That's part of the riddle and why you're needed. Learn his name and you have him."

"I don't want him."

"But if you free him, then he'll finally let me go."

Somehow, Angharad doubted that it would be so simple. She didn't trust her companion. He might appear to be the brother she'd never had—red hair, witch-eyes and all—but there was something feral about him that made her wary. The oak tree caught her gaze again, drawing it in like a snared bird. Still, there was something about that tree, about that house up in its branches. Silence hung about it, thick as cobwebs in a disused tower.

"I'll have to think about this," she said.

Without waiting for Fenn, she crept back through the weeds, keeping low until the first outriding trees of Avalarn Forest shielded her from possible view.

"Why should I believe you?" Angharad asked.

They had returned to where she'd first found him and sat perched on stones like a pair of magpies, facing each other, watching the glitter in each other's eyes and looking for the spark that told of a lie.

"How could I tell you anything but the truth?" Fenn replied. "I'm your friend."

"And if you told me that the world was round—would I be expected to believe that too?"

Fenn laughed. "But it is round, and hangs like an apple in the sky."

"I know," Angharad said, "though there are those that don't." She studied him for another long moment. "So tell me again, what is it you need to be freed from?"

"The wizard."

"I don't see any chains on you."

Fenn tapped his chest. "The bindings are inside—on my heart. That's why I need your song."

"Which can't be sung until the wizard is loosed."

Fenn nodded.

"Tell me this," Angharad said. "If the wizard is set free, what's to stop him from binding me?"

"Gratitude," Fenn replied. "He's been bound a hundred years, treewife. He'll grant any wish to the one who frees him."

Angharad closed her eyes, picturing the tree, its fat bole, the lofty height to its first boughs.

"*You* can't climb it?" she asked.

"It's not a matter of what I'm capable of," Fenn replied. "It's a matter of the geas that was laid on me and the wizard. I can't stray, but I can't enter the house in its branches. And the wizard can't free me until he himself is free. Won't you help us?"

Angharad opened her eyes to find him smiling at her.

"I'll go up the tree," she said, "but I'll make no promises."

"The key to free him—"

"Is in a small wicker basket—the size of a woodsman's fist. I know. You've already told me more than once."

"Oh, treewife, you—"

"I'm *not* a treewife," Angharad said.

She jumped down from her perch on the stones and started for the tree. Fenn hesitated for a long heartbeat, then scrambled down as well to hurry after her.

"How will you get up?" Fenn whispered when they stood directly under the tree.

Though the bark was rough, Angharad didn't trust it to make for safe handholds on a climb up. The bole was too fat for her to shimmy up. She took a coil of rope from her pack and tied a stone to one end.

"Not by witchy means," she said.

The boy stood back as she began to whirl the stone in an ever-widening circle above her head. She hummed to herself, eyes narrowed as she peered up, waiting for just the right moment to cast the stone. Then suddenly it was aloft, flying high, the rope trailing behind it like a long bedraggled tail. Fenn clapped his hands as the stone soared over the lowest branch, then came down the opposite side. Angharad untied the rock. Passing one end of the rope through a slipknot, she pulled it through until the knot was at the branch.

Journeypack and staff stayed by the foot of the tree. With only her small harp on her shoulder, she used the rope to climb up, grunting at the effort it took. Her arms and shoulders were aching long before she reached that first welcome branch, but reach it she did. She sprawled on it and looked down. She saw her belongings, but Fenn was gone. Frowning, she looked up and blinked in amazement. Seen from here, the wizard's refuge was *exactly* like a small house, only set in the branches of a tree instead of on the ground.

Well, I've come this far, Angharad thought. There was

no point in going back down until she'd at least had a look. Besides, her own curiosity was tugging at her now.

She drew up the rope and coiled it carefully around her waist. Without it, she could easily be trapped in this tree. Her witcheries let her talk to the birds and the beasts and to listen to their gossip, but they weren't enough to let her fly off like an eagle, or crawl down the tree trunk like a squirrel.

She made her way up, one branch, then another, moving carefully until she finally clambered up the last to stand on the small porch in front of the door. She laid a hand on the wooden door. The wood was smooth to her touch, the whorls of the grain more intricate than any human artwork could ever be. She turned and looked away.

She could see the breadth of the forest from her vantage point, could watch it sweep into the distance, another sea, green and flowing, twin to the darker waves of gorse and heather that marched westward. Slowly she sank down onto her haunches.

She remembered the foxfire flicker in Fenn's eyes and thought of the lights of Jacky Lantern's marsh-kin who loved to lead travelers astray. Some never came back. She remembered tinker wagons rolling by ruined keeps and how she and the other children would dare each other to go exploring within. Crowen's little brother Broon fell down a shaft in one place and broke his neck. She remembered tales of haunted places where if one spent the night, they were found the next morning either dead, mad, or a poet. This tree had the air of such a place.

She sighed. One hand lifted to the harp at her shoulder. She fingered the smooth length of its small forepillar.

The harp was a gift from Jacky Lantern's kin, as was the music she pulled from its strings. She used it in her journeys through the kingdoms of the Green Isles, to wake the Summerblood where it lay sleeping in folk who had never known they were witches. This was the way the Middle Kingdom survived—by being remembered, by its small magics being served, by the interchange of wisdom and gossip between man and those he shared the world with—the birds, the beasts, the hills, the trees . . .

Poetry was the other third of a bard's spells, she thought. Poetry and harping and the road that led into the green. She had the harp and knew the road. Standing then to face the door, she thought, perhaps I'll find the poetry in here.

She tried the wooden latch and it moved easily under her hand. The door swung open with a push, and she stepped through.

The light was cool and green inside. She stood in the middle of a large room. There were bookshelves with leather-bound volumes on one wall, a worktable on another with bunches of dried herbs hanging above it. A stone hearth stood against another and she wondered what wood even a wizard would dare burn, living here in a tree.

The door closed softly behind her. She turned quickly, half-expecting to see someone there, but she was alone in the room. She walked over to the worktable and ran her hand lightly along its length. There was no dust. And the room itself—it was so big. Bigger than she would have supposed it to be when she was outside.

There was another door by the bookshelves. Curious, she crossed the room and tried its handle. It opened easily as well, leading into another room.

Angharad paused there, a witchy tickle starting up her spine. This was impossible. The house was far too small to have so much space inside. She remembered then the one thing she'd forgotten to ask Fenn. If the wizard had caught him, who had caught the wizard and laid the geas on them both?

She wished now that she had brought her staff with her. The white rowan wood could call up a witch-fire. In a place such as this that had once belonged to a treewizard, fire seemed a good weapon to be carrying. Returning to the work bench, she looked through the herbs and clay jars and bundles of twigs until she found what she was looking for. A rowan sprig. Not much, perhaps, but a fire needed only one spark to start its flames.

Twig in hand, she entered the next room. It was much the same as the first, only more cluttered. Another door led off from it. She went through that door to find yet one more room. This was smaller, a bedchamber with a curtained window and a small table and chair under it. On the table was a small wicker basket.

About the size of a man's fist . . .

She stepped over to the table and picked up the basket. The lid came off easily. Inside was a small bone. A fingerbone, she realized. She closed the basket quickly and looked around. Her witcheries told her that she was no longer alone.

Who are you? a voice breathed in her mind. It seemed to swim out of the walls, a rumbling bass sound, but soft as the last echo of a harp's low strings.

"Who are *you?*" she answered back. No fool she. Names were power.

She felt what could only be a smile form in her mind. *I am the light on a hawk's wings, the whisper of a tree's boughs, the smell of bell heather, the texture of loam. I dream like a longstone, run like a fox, dance like the wind.*

"You're the wizard, then," Angharad said. Only wizards used a hundred words where one would do. Except for their spells. Then all they needed was the one name.

Why are you here?

"To free you."

Again that smile took shape in her mind. *And who told you that I need to be freed?*

"The boy in the forest—the one you've bound. Fenn."

The boy is a liar.

Angharad sighed. She'd thought as much, really. So why *was* she here? To spend the night and see if she'd wake mad or a poet, or not wake at all? But when she spoke, all she said was, "And perhaps you are the liar."

The presence in her mind laughed. *Perhaps I am,* it said. *Lie down on the bed, dear guest. I want to show you something.*

"I can see well enough standing up, thank you all the same."

And if you fall down and crack your head when the vision comes—who will you blame?

Angharad made a slow circuit around the room, stopping when she came to the bed. She touched its coverlet, poked at the mattress. Sighing, she kept a firm hold of the basket in one hand, the rowan twig in the other, and lay down. No sooner did her head touch the pillow, than the coverlet rose up in a twist and bound her limbs, holding her fast.

"You *are* a liar," she said, trying to keep the edge of panic out of her voice.

Or you are a fool, her captor replied.

"At least let me see you."

I have something different in mind, dear guest. Something else to show you.

Before Angharad could protest, before she could light the rowan twig with her witcheries, the presence in her mind wrapped her in its power and took her away.

6

THE PERSPECTIVE SHE had was that of a bird. She was high in the oak that held the treewizard's house, higher than a man or woman could climb, higher than a child, amongst branches so slender they would scarcely take the weight of a squirrel. The view that vantage point gave her was breathtaking—the endless sweep of forest and moor, striding off in opposite directions. The sky, huge above her, close enough to touch. The ground so far below it was another world.

She had no body. She was merely a presence, like the presence inside the treewizard's house, hovering in the air. A disembodied ghost.

Watch, a now-familiar voice said.

Give me back my body, she told it.

First you must watch.

Her perspective changed, bringing her closer to the ground, and she saw a young man who looked vaguely familiar approaching the tree. He looked like a tinker, red-haired, bright clothes and all, but she could tell by the bundle of books that joined the journeypack on his back that he was a scholar.

He came to learn, her captor told her.

Nothing wrong with that, she replied. *Knowledge is a good thing to own. It allows you to understand the world around you better and no one can take it away from you.*

A good thing, perhaps, her captor agreed, *depending on what one plans to do with it.*

The young man was cutting footholds into the tree with a small axe. Angharad could feel the tree shiver with each blow.

Doesn't he understand what he's doing to the tree? she asked.

All he understands is his quest for knowledge. He plans to become the most powerful wizard of all.

But why?

A good question. I don't doubt he wishes now that he'd thought it all through more clearly before he came.

Angharad wanted to pursue that further, but by now the young man had reached the porch. He had a triumphant look on his face as he stood before the door. Grinning, he shoved open the door and strode inside. The presence in Angharad's mind tried to draw her in after him, but she was too busy watching the footholds that the young man had cut into the tree grow back, one by one, until there was no sign that they'd ever been there. Then she drifted inside.

Look at him, her captor said.

She did. He'd thrown his packs down on the floor and was pulling out the books in the treewizard's library, tossing each volume on the floor after only the most cursory glances.

"I've done it," he was muttering. "Sweet Dath, I've found a treasure trove."

He tossed the book he was holding down, then got up to investigate the next room. After he'd gone, the books on the floor rose one by one and returned to their places. Angharad hurried in after the young man to find him already in the third room, dancing an awkward jig, his boots clattering on the floorboards.

"I'll show them all!" he sang. "I'll have such power that they'll all bow down to me. They'll come to me with their troubles and, if they're rich enough, if they catch me in an amiable mood, I might even help them." He rubbed his hands together. "Won't I be fine, won't I just."

He was not well looked-upon, her captor explained. *He wanted so much and had so little, and wasn't willing to work for what he did want. He needed it all at once.*

I understand now, Angharad said. *He's—*

Watch.

Days passed in a flicker, showing the young man growing increasingly impatient with the slow speed at which he gained his knowledge.

It was still work after all, Angharad's captor said.

"Damn this place!" the young man roared one morning. He flung the book he was studying across the room. "Where is the magic? Where is the power?" He strode back and forth, running a hand through the tangled knots of his hair.

Can't he feel it? Angharad asked. *It's in every book, every nook and cranny of this place. The whole tree positively reeks of it.*

She felt her captor smile inside her mind, a weary smile. *He has yet to understand the difference between what is taken and what is given,* he explained.

Angharad thought of ghostly harpers in a marsh, Jacky Lantern's kin, pressing a harp into her hands. Not until she'd been ready to give up what she wanted most— as misguided a seeking after power as this young man's was—had she received a wisdom she hadn't even been aware she was looking for.

She watched in horror now as the young man began

to pile the books in a heap in the center of the room. He took flint and steel from his pocket and bent over them.

No! Angharad cried, forgetting that this was the past she was being shown. *We can't let him!*

Too late, her captor said. *The deed's long past and done. But watch. The final act has yet to play.*

As the young man bent over the books, the room about him came alive. Chairs flowed into snake-like shapes and caught him by the ankles, pulling him down to the floor. A worktable spilled clay jars and herb bundles about the room as it lunged towards him, folding over his body, suddenly as pliable as a blanket.

Flint fell with a clatter in one direction, steel in another. The young man screamed. The room exploded into a whirlwind of furniture and books and debris, spinning faster and faster, until Angharad grew ill looking at it. Then, just as suddenly as it had come up, the wind died down. The room blurred, mists swelled within its confines, grew tattered, dissolved. When it was gone, the room looked no different than it had when Angharad had first entered it herself. The young man was gone.

Where . . . ? she began.

Inside the tree, her captor told her. *Trapped forever and a day, or until a mage or a witch should come to answer the riddle.*

Before Angharad could ask, the presence in her mind whisked her away and the next thing she knew she was lying in the bed once more, the coverlet lying slack and unmoving. She sat up slowly, clutching basket and rowan twig in her hands.

"What is the riddle?" she asked the empty room.

Who is wiser, the presence in her mind asked: *the man who knows everything, or the man who knows nothing?*

"Neither," Angharad replied correctly. "Is that it? Is that all?"

Oh, no, the presence told her. *You must tell me my name.*

Angharad opened the wicker basket and looked

down at the tiny fingerbone. "The wizard in the tree— his name is Fenn. The boy I met is what he could be, should he live again. But you—you live in the tree and if you have need of a name, it would be Druswid." It was a word in the old tongue that meant the knowledge of the oak. "Puretongue was your student," she added, "wasn't he?"

A long time ago, the presence in her mind told her. *But we learned from each other. You did well, dear guest. Sleep now.*

Angharad tried to shake off the drowsiness that came over her, but to no avail. It crept through her body in a wearying wave. She fell back onto the bed, fell into a dreamless sleep.

When Angharad woke, it was dawn and she was lying at the foot of the giant oak tree. She sat up, surprisingly not at all stiff from her night on the ground, and turned to find Fenn sitting cross-legged beside her pack and staff, watching her. Angharad looked up at the house, high in the tree.

"How did I get down?" she asked.

Fenn shrugged. He played with a small bone that hung around his neck by a thin leather thong. Angharad looked down at her hands to find she was holding the rowan twig in the one, and the basket in the other. She opened the basket, but the fingerbone was gone.

"A second chance," she said to Fenn. "Is that what you've been given?"

He nodded. "A second chance."

"What will you do with it?"

He grinned. "Go back up that tree and learn, but for all the right reasons this time."

"And what would they be?"

"Don't you know, treewife?"

"I'm *not* a treewife."

"Oh, no? Then how did you guess Druswid's name?"

"I didn't guess. I'm a witch, Fenn—that gives me a certain sight."

Fenn's eyes widened slightly with a touch of awe. "You actually saw Druswid?"

Angharad shook her head. "But I know a tree's voice when I hear it. And who else would be speaking to me from an oak tree? Not a wet-eared impatient boy who wanted to be a wizard for all the wrong reasons."

"You're angry because I tricked you into going up into the tree. But I didn't lie. I just didn't tell you everything."

"Why not?"

"I didn't think you'd help me."

Angharad gathered up her harp and pack and swung them onto her back. Fenn handed her her staff.

"Well?" he asked. "Would you have?"

Angharad looked up at the tree. "I'm not dead," she said, "and I don't feel mad, so perhaps I've become a poet."

"Treewi—"Fenn paused as Angharad swung her head towards him. "Angharad," he said. "*Would* you have helped me?"

"Probably," she said. "But not for the right reasons." She leaned over to him and gave him a kiss on the brow. "Good luck, Fenn."

"My song," he said. "You never gave me my song."

"You never needed a song."

"But I'd like one now. Please?"

So Angharad sang to him before she left, a song of the loneliness that wisdom can sometimes bring—when the student won't listen, when the form is bound to the earth by its roots and only the mind ranges free. A loneliness grown from a world where magic as a way of life lay forgotten under too many quests for power. She called it "The Weeping Oak" and she only sang it that once and never again. But there was a poetry in it that her songs had never had before.

When she left Fenn to his studies in the wizard's oak, that poetry took wing in the songs that she sung to the accompaniment of her harp. It joined the two parts of a bard that she already had, slipping into her life as neatly as an otter's path through the river's water. She continued to range far and wide, as tinkers will, but she was a red-haired witch, following a bard's road into the green, which is another way of saying she was content with what she had.

7

RUTNER SPENN STOOD under the awning of Boyll's Meat Mart and scanned the noon crowds that filled Carlisle's market square. He was a rounded individual with a head like a moon, thin limbs sprouting from a figure that appeared to have taken the mold for its shape from a child's ball. His bald pate gleamed in the sun when he stepped forward, thinking he'd seen the man he was looking for, but he stepped back under the awning once more when he saw his mistake.

The market was a hubbub of activity. Merchants, farmers and fishwives cried their wares, customers argued the prices. There were singers on two of the square's corners, jugglers on the third, a storyteller on the fourth.

If it existed, it was available in Carlisle. The town was a free state trading center set on a small island just off the Festian coast, connected to the mainland by three bridges and a ferry service. Northward, war raged as the Allies fought the Saramand, but judging by the uninterrupted commerce and jollity in Carlisle's streets, one would think that the war never existed—and certainly one would not realize that the enemy lines lay a scant hundred miles north of the town.

But listening closely, farmers could be overheard complaining of the troop movements through their fields, and here and there in a sheltered alleyway, ragged figures could be seen stirring as the day wore on, missing a limb or an eye, their tattered clothing the familiar mottled green and brown of the Allies' foot soldiers.

Spenn had no time for either. The man he sought was neither a veteran nor a farmer. Impatience nattered in Spenn's thoughts and he had to forcibly concentrate on not shifting his weight restlessly from one foot to another. It would not do for potential customers to see his impatience, but he couldn't help worrying. He'd been away from his own shop for a good half-hour now and who knew what poor bargains his wife had made in the time he was gone. The woman had no head for business.

Just as he was seriously considering his return, he spotted his man.

"Kellin!" he called through the crowd.

Browdie Kellin was as thin as Spenn was stout. The fine cut of his clothes hung untidily from his rake's frame, his disheveled appearance only accentuated by the wild mass of curly brown hair that topped his stoat-featured face.

Spenn relaxed, his impatience forgotten as Kellin made his way through the crowd.

"Are you still acquiring odd curios?" Spenn asked when the other man had joined him under the awning.

"My principal is still interested in such items," Kellin allowed.

Spenn smiled. "And is he still carefully cloaking himself in anonymity?"

"He is," Kellin agreed. He looked pointedly at the basket by Spenn's feet. "What do you have for us?"

"Not here," Spenn said. "Come by the shop after closing. And bring a heavy purse. What I have for you is rare beyond your imagining."

"What—"

Spenn shook his head, cutting Kellin off. "This is not the place for such discussions," he said. "Come by after closing. You won't regret it."

With that, he hefted his basket and walked off, leaving Kellin under the awning, his curiosity suitably piqued.

Kellin didn't make his appearance until mid-evening, but Spenn's impatience was completely fled by then. Once the hook was in, he could spend a month in dickering and discussion without any need for hurry. He dealt in antiques and curios, so most of his items were one of a kind. When he knew the customer for a particular piece, he no longer fretted about the time it took to strike the deal. All that was important was for how much the item was finally sold.

His wife was in their apartment above the store when he let Kellin in and ushered the lanky man into the back room. There were two seats set on either side of a small lacquered wood table there. On the table was a lantern, a tray with two china mugs and a teapot, and a lead box.

Once they were seated, Spenn poured them each a serving of tea, then opened the lid of the box to take out a small square-shaped object, wrapped in silk and tied shut with braided goat's hair. He set the object beside Kellin's tea mug.

"What is it?" Kellin asked. "And how much?"

Spenn shook his head. "Look first, then we'll talk."

He watched Kellin's face as he undid the braiding and folded back the silk to reveal an ebony puzzle-box inlaid with silver patterning. He smiled as Kellin began to trace a finger along the silver pattern, shivering and putting it quickly down. Spenn knew what Kellin had just felt—a dark shadowy whisper in the back of his mind that cat-pawed up and down his spine. He knew, for he'd experienced the exact same sensation when he'd purchased the item. The puzzle-box made him uneasy for no reason he could fathom; but that very uneasiness was what had let him understand just what it was that had fallen into his hands.

Kellin's gaze rose to meet Spenn's. "What is it?" he asked again, but this time his voice held the proper note of awe.

"Wizard's work," Spenn said. "And it's old—you can tell your principal that. Incredibly old. I can't even begin to date it."

Kellin nodded, then cleared his throat. "Ah . . ."

Spenn understood immediately. He wrapped the puzzle-box once more, tied off the braiding, then replaced it in its lead container. As soon as he closed the lid, the room seemed brighter. Shadows withdrew and it was easier to breathe. Spenn felt uncomfortable each time he exposed the object, but he knew the surest way to sell its authenticity was for the buyer to experience its discomfort firsthand, *before* the bargaining began.

"Lead blocks the influence of witcheries," he explained.

Kellin nodded as though he'd always been aware of that—something that Spenn doubted; but he let it pass.

"How did you acquire it?" Kellin asked.

"From one of my agents in Sauwait. The artifact itself was found in one of the lost cities of the Kharanan. Apparently a Khohr tribesman discovered it in a tower that was uncovered for a day or two before the sands swallowed it again."

"Are you saying that this is an authentic Kharanan artifact? That it predates the coming of the sands?"

Spenn nodded.

"Impossible."

Spenn merely reached for the lid of the lead container once more, pausing when Kellin shook his head.

Smiling again, Spenn picked up his tea mug instead. He took a sip and regarded Kellin over the brim of the mug.

"You felt its power," he said as he set the mug back down on the table beside the lead container. "That could come from no reproduction."

"Yes, but the ancient Kharanan civilizations . . . they're no more than legends."

Spenn shrugged. "Perhaps. Let me remind you of another legend. Did your mam ever tell you the story of Fair Lazny?"

Kellin slowly nodded. "He killed the Witch Queen of the Graen."

"Do you remember how he did it?"

A frown furrowed Kellin's brow before he replied. "With a magical artifact—a child's top that, when it was spun, created a pattern in the air that swallowed the Witch Queen."

"Such artifacts were called *glascrow,*" Spenn said. "There were any number of them it seems, if the old tales are to be believed. There was a dagger, a bowl, a spear, a child's hoop . . ."

"How do you know this?"

"It's my business to know such things."

Kellin nodded. "Fair enough. And you believe that this"—he indicated the lead container with a movement of his chin—"is one such object?"

"I'm convinced of it."

Kellin said nothing for a long moment.

"Your principal . . . ?" Spenn prompted.

"Is quite interested in such things," Kellin admitted. "How much?"

"Ten thousand—in gold."

"Impossible!"

Spenn shrugged. He'd take a third of that and still make a tidy profit, but he had no intention of letting Kellin know that.

"I have others interested in such items," he said. "I came to you first because your principal has provided me with a good business over the past year, but if the price is too steep . . ."

"Five thousand," Kellin said.

Spenn merely laughed.

Kellin would buy. Spenn had no doubt of that. All that remained now was to enjoy the bargaining.

8

MOSTLY, WHEN ANGHARAD played the small harp she'd named Garrow, she pulled dance tunes from its strings, lilting jigs or reels that set feet tapping until the floorboards shook and the rafters rang. But some nights the memory of old sorrows returned. Lying in wait like marsh mists, they clouded her eyes with their arrival. On those nights, the music she pulled from Garrow's metal-wound strings was more bitter than sweet, slow airs that made the heart regret and brought unbidden memories to haunt the minds of those who listened.

"Enough of that," the innkeeper said.

The tune faltered and Angharad looked up into his angry face. She lay her hands across the strings, stilling the harp's plaintive singing.

"I said you could make music," the innkeeper told her, "not drive my customers away."

It took Angharad a few moments to return from that place in her memory where the music had brought her to this inn where her body sat, drawing the music from the strings of her harp. The common room was half-empty and oddly subdued, whereas earlier every table had been filled and men stood shoulder-to-shoulder at the bar, joking and telling each other ever more embroidered tales. The few who spoke now did so in hushed voices; fewer still would meet her gaze.

"You'll have to go," the innkeeper said, his voice not so harsh now. She saw in his eyes that he too was remembering a forgotten sorrow.

"I . . ."

How to tell him that on nights such as these, the sorrow came, whether she willed it or not? That if she had her choice she would rather forget as well?

Sometimes the memories the music woke were not so gay and charming. They hurt. Yet such memories served a purpose, too, as the music knew well. They helped to break the circles of history so that mistakes weren't repeated. But how was she to explain such things to this tall, grim-faced innkeeper who'd been looking only for an evening's entertainment for his customers? How to put into words what only music could tell?

"I . . . I'm sorry," she said.

He nodded, almost sympathetically. Then his eyes grew hard. "Just go."

She made no protest. She knew what she was—tinker, witch and harper. This far south of Kellmidden, only the latter allowed her much acceptance with those who traveled a road just to get from here to there, rather than for the sake of the traveling itself. For the sake of the road that led into the green, where poetry and harping met to sing of the Middle Kingdom.

Standing, she swung the harp up on one shoulder, her small journeypack on the other. At the door she collected her staff of white rowan wood. Witches' wood. Not until the door swung closed behind her did the usual level of conversation and laughter return to the common room.

But they would remember. Her. The music. There was one man who watched her from a corner, face dark with brooding. She meant to leave before they remembered other things. Before one or another wondered aloud if it was true that witch's skin burned at the touch of cold iron—as did that of the kowrie folk.

As she stepped away from the door, a huge shadowed shape arose from where it had been crouching by a window. The quick beat of her pulse only sharpened when she saw that it was a man—a misshapen man. His chest was massive, his arms and legs like small trees. But a hump rose from his back, and his head jutted almost from his chest at an awkward angle. His legs were bowed as though his weight was almost too much for them. He shuffled, rather than walked, as he closed the short space between them.

Light from the window spilled across his features. One eye was set higher in that broad face than the other. The nose had been broken—more than once. His hair was a knotted thicket, his beard a bird's nest of matted tangles.

Angharad began to bring her staff between them. The white rowan wood could call up a witch-fire that was good for little more than calling up a flame in a damp campfire, but it could startle. That might be enough for her to make her escape.

The monstrous man reached a hand towards her. "Puh-pretty," he said.

Before Angharad could react, there came a quick movement from around the side of the inn.

"Go on!" the newcomer cried. It was the barmaid from the inn, a slender blue-eyed girl whose blonde hair hung in one thick braid across her breast. The innkeeper had called her Jessa. "Get away from her, you big oaf." She made a shooing motion with her hand.

Angharad saw something flicker briefly in the man's eyes as he turned. A moment of shining light. A flash of regret. She realized then that he'd been speaking of her music, not her. He'd been reaching to touch the harp, not her. She wanted to call him back, but the barmaid was thrusting a package wrapped in unbleached cotton at her. The man had shambled away, vanishing into the darkness in the time it took Angharad to look from the package to where he'd been standing.

"Something for the road," Jessa said. "It's not much—some cheese and bread."

"Thank you," Angharad replied. "That man . . . ?"

"Oh, don't mind him. That's only Pog—the village half-wit. Fael lets him sleep in the barn in return for what work he can do around the inn." She smiled suddenly. "He's seen the kowrie folk, he has. To hear him tell it—and you'd need the patience of one of Dath's priests to let him get the tale out—they dance all round the stones on a night such as this."

"What sort of a night is this?"

"Full moon."

Jessa pointed eastward. Rising above the trees there, Angharad saw the moon rising, swollen and round above the trees. She remembered a circle of old longstones that she'd passed on the road that took her to the inn. They stood far off from the road on a hill overlooking the Grey Sea, a league or so west of the village. Old stones, like silent sentinels, watching the distant waves. A place where kowrie would dance, she thought, if they were so inclined.

"You should go," Jessa said.

Angharad gave her a questioning look.

The barmaid nodded towards the inn. "They're talking about witches in there, and spells laid with music. They're not bad men, but any man who drinks . . ."

Angharad nodded. A hard day's work, then drinking all night. To some it was enough to excuse any deed. They were honest folk, after all. Not tinkers. Not witches.

She touched Jessa's arm. "Thank you."

"We're both women," the barmaid said with a smile. "We have to stick together, now don't we?" Her features, half-hidden in the gloom, grew more serious as she added, "Stay off the road if you can. Depending on how things go . . . well, there's some as have horses."

Angharad thought of a misshapen man and a place of standing stones, of moonlight and dancing kowrie.

"I will," she said.

Jessa gave her another quick smile, then slipped once more around the corner of the inn. Angharad listened to her quiet footfalls as she ran back to the kitchen. Giving the inn a considering look, she stuffed the barmaid's gift of food into her journeypack and set off down the road, staff in hand.

9

THERE WERE MANY tales told of the menhirs and
stone circles that dotted the kingdoms of the Green Isles.
Wizardfolk named them holy places, sacred to the Summerlord; reservoirs where the old powers of hill and
moon could be gathered by the rites of dhruides and the
like. The priests of Dath named them evil and warned all
to shun their influence. The common folk were merely
wary of them—viewing them as neither good nor evil, but
rather places where mysteries lay too deep for ordinary
folk.

And there *was* mystery in them, Anghared thought.

From where she stood, she could see their tall fingers
silhouetted against the sky. Mists lay thick about their
hill—drawn up from the sea that murmured a stone's
throw or two beyond. The moon was higher now; the
night as still as an inheld breath. Expectant. Anghared
left the road to approach the stone circle where Pog
claimed the kowrie danced on nights of the full moon.
Nights when her harp played older musics than she
knew, drawing the airs more from the wind, it seemed,
than the flesh and bone that held the instrument and
plucked its strings.

The bracken was damp underfoot. In no time at all, her bare legs were wet. She circled around two stone outcrops, her route eventually bringing her up the hill from the side facing the sea. The murmur of its waves was very clear now. The sharp tang of its salt was in the mist. Angharad couldn't see below her waist for that mist, but the hilltop was clear. And the stones.

They rose high above her, four times her height, grey and weathered. Before she entered their circle, she dropped her journeypack and staff to the ground. From its sheath on the inside of her jerkin, she took out a small knife and left that as well. If this was a place to which the kowrie came, she knew they would have no welcome for one bearing cold iron. Lastly, she unbuttoned her shoes and removed her jerkin, setting them beside her pack. Only then did she enter the circle, in pleated skirt and blouse, barefoot, with only her harp in hand.

She wasn't surprised to find the hunchback from the village inside the circle. He was perched on the kingstone, short legs dangling.

"Hello, Pog," she said.

She had no fear of him as she crossed the circle to where he sat. There was more kinship between them than either might claim outside this circle. Their Summerblood bound them.

"Huh-huh-huh . . ." Frustration tightened every line of his body as he struggled to shape the word. "Huh-low . . ."

Angharad stepped close and laid her hand against his cheek. She wondered, what songs were held prisoner by that stumbling tongue? For she could see a poetry in his eyes, denied its voice. A longing, given no release.

"Will you sing for me, Pog?" she asked. "Will you help me call the stones to dance?"

The eagerness in his nod almost made her weep. But it was not for pity that she was here tonight. It was to commune with a kindred spirit. He caught her hand with his and she gave it a squeeze before gently freeing her fingers. She sat at the foot of the stone and brought her harp around to her lap. Pog was awkward as he scrambled down from his perch to sit where he could watch her.

Fingers to strings. Once, softly, one after the other, to test the tuning. And then she began to play.

It was the same music that the instrument had offered at the inn, but in this place it soared so freely that there could be no true comparison. There was nothing to deaden the ringing of the strings here. No stone walls and wooden roof. No metal furnishings and trappings. No hearts that had to be tricked into listening.

The moon was directly overhead now and the music resounded between it and the sacred hill of the stone circle. It woke echoes like the skirling of pipes, like the thunder of hooves on sod. It woke lights in the old grey stones—flickering glimmers that sparked from one tall menhir to the other. It woke a song so bright in Angharad's heart that her chest hurt. It woke a dance in her companion so that he rose to his feet and shuffled between the stones.

Pog sang as he moved, a tuneless singing that made strange harmonies with Angharad's harping. Against the moonlight of her harp notes, it was the sound of earth shifting, stones grinding. When it took on the bass timbre of a stag's belling call, Angharad thought she saw antlers rising from his brow, the tines pointing skyward to the moon like the menhir. His back was straighter as he danced, the hump gone.

It's Hafarl, Angharad thought, awestruck. The Summerlord's possessed him.

Their music grew more fierce, a wild exultant sound that rang between the stones. The sparking flickers of light moved so quickly they were like streaming ribbons, bright as moonlight. The mist scurried in between the stones, swirling in its own dance, so that more often than not Angharad could only catch glimpses of the antlered dancing figure. His movements were liquid, echoing each rise and fall of the music. Angharad's heart reached out to him. He was—

Something struck her across the head. The music faltered, stumbled, then died as her harp was knocked from her grip. A hand grabbed one of her braids and hauled her to her feet.

"Do you see? Did you hear?" a harsh voice demanded.

Angharad could see them now—men from the inn. Their voices were loud in the sudden silence. Their shapes exaggerated, large and threatening in the mist.

"We see, Macal."

It was the one named Macal who had struck her. Who had watched her so intently in the common room of the inn. Who held her by her braid. Who hit her again. He stank of sweat and strong drink. And fear.

"Calling down a curse on us, she was," Macal cried. "And what better place than these damned stones?"

Other men gripped her now. They shackled her wrists with cold iron and pulled her from the circle by a chain attached to those shackles. She fell to her knees and looked back. There was no sign of Pog, no sign of anything but her harp, lying on its side near the kingstone. The men dragged her to her feet.

"Leave me alo—"she began, finally finding her voice.

Macal hit her a third time. "You'll not speak again, witch. Not till the priest questions you. Understand?"

They tore cloth strips from her skirt then to gag her. They tore open her blouse and fondled and pinched her as they dragged her back to town. They threw her into the small storage room of the village's mill. Four stone walls. A door barred on the outside by a wooden beam, slotted in place. Two drunk men for guards outside, laughing and singing.

It took a long time for Angharad to lift her bruised body up from the stone floor and work free the gag. She closed her blouse somewhat by tying together the shirt tails. She hammered at the door with her shackled fists. There was no answer. Finally she sank to her knees and laid her head against the wall. She closed her eyes, trying to recapture the moment before this horror began, but all she could recall was the journey from the stone circle to this prison. The cruel men and the joy they took from her pain.

Then she thought of Pog. . . . Had they captured him as well? When she tried to bring his features to mind, all that came was an image of a stag on a hilltop, bellowing at the moon. She could see . . .

The stag. Pog. Changed into an image of Hafarl by the music. Left as a stag in the stone circle by the intrusion of the men from the inn who'd come, cursing and drunk, to find themselves a witch. The men hadn't seen him. But as Angharad's assailants dragged her from the stone circle, grey-clad shapes stepped from the stones, where time held them bound except for nights such as this when the moon was full.

They were kowrie, thin and wiry, with narrow dark-skinned faces and feral eyes. Their dark hair was braided with shells and feathers; their jerkins, trousers, boots and cloaks were the grey of the stones. One by one, they stepped out into the circle until there were as many of them as there were stones. Thirteen kowrie. The stag bellowed at the moon, a trumpeting sound. The kowrie touched Angharad's harp with fingers thin as rowan twigs.

"Gone now," one said, her voice a husky whisper.

Another drew a plaintive note from Angharad's harp. "Music stolen, moonlight spoiled," he said.

A third laid her narrow hands on the stag's trembling flanks. "Lead us to her, Summerborn," she said.

Other kowrie approached the beast.

"The cold iron bars us from their dwellings," one said.

Another nodded. "But not you."

"Lead us to her."

"Open their dwellings to us."

"We were but waking."

"We missed our dance."

"A hundred moons without music."

"We would hear her harp."

"We would follow our kin."

"Into the green."

The green, where poetry and harping met and opened a door to the Middle Kingdom. The stag pawed at the ground, hearing the need in their voices. It lifted its antlered head, snorting at the sky. The men. Where had they taken her? The stag remembered a place where men dwelt in houses set close to each other. There was pain in that place . . .

Angharad opened her eyes. What had she seen? A dream? Pog, with that poetry in his eyes, become a stag, surrounded by feral-eyed kowrie. . . . She pushed herself away from the wall and sat on her haunches, shackled wrists held on her lap before her. The stone walls of her prison bound her. The cold chains weighed her down. Still, her heart beat, her thoughts were her own. Her voice had not been taken from her.

She began to sing.

It was the music of hill and moon, a calling-down music, keening and wild. There was a stag's lowing in it, the murmur of sea against shore. There was moonlight in it and the slow grind of earth against stone. There was harping in it, and the sound of the wind as it sped across the gorse-backed hills.

On a night such as this, she thought, there was no stilling such music. It was not bound by walls or shackles. It ran free, out from her prison, out of the village; into the night, into the hills. It was heard there, by kowrie and stag. It was heard closer as well.

From the faraway place that the music took her, Angharad heard the alarm raised outside her prison. The wooden beam scraping as it was drawn from the door. The door was pushed open and the small chamber where her body sat singing grew bright from the glare of torches. But she was hardly even there anymore. She was out on the hills, running with the stag and the kowrie, leading them to her with her song, one more ghostly shape in the mist that was rolling down into the village.

"St-stop that, you," one of the guards said. His unease was plain in voice and stance. Like his companion, he was suddenly sober.

Angharad heard him, but only from a great distance. Her music never faltered.

The two guards kept to the doorway, staring at her, unsure of what to do. Then Macal was there, with his hatred of witches, and they followed his lead. He struck her until she fell silent, but the music carried on, from her heart into the night, inaudible to these men, but growing louder when they dragged her out. The earth underfoot resounded like a drumskin with her silent song. The moonlit sky above trembled.

"Bring wood," Macal called as he pulled her along the ground by her chains. "We'll burn her now."

"But the priest . . ." one of the men protested.

Macal glared at the man. "If we wait for him, she'll have us all enspelled. We'll do it now."

No one moved. Other villagers were waking now—
Fael the innkeeper and the barmaid Jessa; the miller
roused first by Angharad's singing, now coming to see to
what use Macal had put his mill; fishermen, grumpy, for
it was still hours before dawn, when they'd rise to set their
nets out past the shoals; the village goodwives. They
looked at the red-haired woman, lying on the ground at
Macal's feet, her body bruised, her hands shackled, the
chains in Macal's hands. His earlier supporters backed
away from him.

"Have you gone mad?" the miller demanded of him.

Macal pointed at Angharad. "Dath damn you, are you
blind? She's a witch. She's casting a spell on us all. Can't
you smell the stink of it in the air?"

"Let her go," the innkeeper said quietly.

Macal shook his head and drew his sword. "Fire's
best—it burns the magic from them—but a sword can do
the job as well."

The mist was entering the village now, roiling down
the streets, filled with ghostly running shapes. Lifting her
head from the ground, Angharad saw the kowrie, saw the
stag. She looked at her captor and suddenly understood
what drove him to his hate of witches. He had the Summerblood in his veins too.

"There . . . there's no need for this," she said. "We
are kin . . ."

But Macal didn't hear her. He was staring into the
mist. He saw the flickering shapes of the kowrie. And towering over them all he saw the stag, its tined antlers
gleaming in the moonlight, the poetry in its eyes that
burned like a fire. He dropped the chains and ran towards the beast, swinging his sword two-handedly. Villagers ran to intercept him, but they were too late. Macal's
sword bit deep into the stag's throat.

The beast stumbled to its knees, spraying blood.
Macal lifted his blade for a second stroke, but strong

hands wrestled the sword from him. When he tried to rise, the villagers struck him with their fists.

"Murderer!" the miller cried.

"He never did you harm!"

"It was a beast!" Macal cried. "A demon beast—summoned by the witch!"

They let him rise then to see what he'd slain. Pog lay there, gasping his last breath, the poetry dying in his eyes. Only Macal and Angharad with their Summerblood had seen a stag. To the villagers, Macal had struck down their village half-wit who'd never done a hurtful thing.

"I . . ." Macal began taking a step forward, but the villagers pushed him away.

The mists swirled thick around him. Only he and Angharad could see the flickering grey shapes that moved in it, feral eyes gleaming, slender fingers pinching and nipping at his skin. He fled, running headlong between the houses. The mist clotted around him as he reached the outskirts of the village. A great wind rushed down from the hills. Hafarl's breath, Angharad thought, watching.

The wind tore away the mists. She saw the kowrie flee with it, thirteen slender shapes running into the hills. Where Macal had fallen, only a squat stone lay that looked for all the world like a crouching man, arms and legs drawn in close to his body. It had not been there before.

The villagers shaped the Sign of Horns to ward themselves. Angharad held out her shackled arms to the innkeeper. Silently he fetched the key from one of Macal's companions. Just as silently Angharad pointed to the men who had attacked her in the stone circle. She met their shamed gazes, one by one, then pointed to where Pog lay.

She waited while they fetched a plank and rolled Pog's body onto it. When they were ready, she led the way out of the village to the stone circle, the men following. Not until they had delivered their burden to the hilltop stones did she speak.

"Go now."

They left at a run. Angharad stood firm until they were out of sight, then slowly she sank to her knees beside the body. Laying her head on its barreled chest, she wept.

It was the kowrie who hollowed the ground under the kingstone and laid Pog there. And it was the kowrie who pressed the small harp into Angharad's hands and bade her play. She could feel no joy in this music that her fingers pulled from the strings. The magic was gone. But she played all the same, head bent over her instrument while the kowrie moved amongst the stones in a slow dance to honor the dead.

Mists grew thick again. Then a hoofbeat brought Angharad's head up. Her music faltered. The stag stood there watching her, the poetry alive in its eyes.

"Are you truly there?" she asked the beast. "Or are you but a phantom I've called up to ease my heart?"

The stag stepped forward and pressed a wet nose against her cheek. She stroked its neck. The hairs were coarse. There was no doubt that this was flesh and muscle under her hand. When the stag stepped away, she began to play once more. The music grew of its own accord under her fingers, that wild exultant music that was bitter and sweet, all at once.

Between her music and the poetry in the stag's eyes, Angharad sensed the membrane that separated this world from the Middle Kingdoms of the kowrie growing thin. So thin. Like mist. One by one the dancing kowrie passed through, thirteen grey-cloaked figures with teeth gleaming white in their dark faces as they smiled and stepped from this world to the one beyond. Last to go was the stag; he gave her one final look, the poetry shining in his eyes, then stepped away. The music stilled in Angharad's fingers. The harp fell silent. They were gone now, Pog and his kowrie. Gone from this hill, from this world.

Stepped away.

Into the green.

Hugging her harp to her chest, Angharad waited for the rising sun to wash over the old stone circle and tried not to feel so alone.

10

ALTHOUGH SHE NO longer had a wagon, nor a tinker company to travel with, the blood of a traveler ran too thickly through Angharad's veins for her to ever surrender the road for a settled life. She was like the migrating birds—no matter where she found herself, one day she simply had to up and go. Down that path. Up that lane. The road never eased its hold on her.

She traveled the length and breadth of the Green Isles, wintering once in the West Marches of Ardmeyn, cozily ensconced in the smoky caves of the diminutive Tus, the dark air rich with the smell of burning peat; summering on the Isle of Morennen, camped in sight of Horn Henge with the moors a sea of heather on three sides, and the Channel Sea a deep perfect blue on the fourth; a spring in Nowe, when the marshes were a riot of color and birds; an autumn in Umbria, riding the riverboats of the Longswaying from its mouth in Traws to its source in Cermyn.

When the road took her through Cermyn, she always stopped at the Druswid Oak in Avalarn to guest with the treewizard's apprentice, Fenn. The feral child she'd once known had grown into a fairly sober young man—no stranger to humor, but given a second chance as he had been, he took his studies far more seriously now. Her arrival—always expected, for all that she often didn't know she was coming herself until she was there—signaled a time for Fenn to put aside his books and lessons and take a well-deserved holiday.

They would ramble through the forest and its surrounding hills, gossiping with the badgers and squirrels, the ravens and hares. And with each other. Though the only blood-tie that lay between them was Hafarl's gift, they felt more like brother and sister than many born of the same mother. The joy in Fenn's face when he saw her coming—spreading through him like ripples expanding from a stone dropped in water—would turn into whoops of joy as he ran to meet her.

But not this year.

This year he stood at the foot of the oak, his face grave as he toyed nervously with the fingerbone that hung from a leather thong about his neck.

His mood leapt to her, Summerblood to Summerblood, swift as a vanishing otter, so that she approached him anxiously, questions forming in her eyes before she could voice them.

"It's bad," he said.

"What is?" Angharad asked. "Fenn, what is it?"

But he wouldn't answer, not until they were in his house, high in the tree, with the wind talking in the boughs and Fenn's home swaying slightly in the branches. There he took her to a worktable and showed her his brass scryer. The water in it lay still as stone. The image it disclosed was of a small silver and ebony box, ornately designed, a mingling pattern of dark and light that stole the gaze and trapped it fast.

"It doesn't go away," Fenn said.

Angharad looked for as long as she could, but the box's design disturbed her. The more she looked, the more her head spun. It was like hanging over the edge of a cliff, high above the sea, and suddenly realizing that there were no handholds. The design drew her into it, the strange mix of linework and geometric spirals catching her gaze like a fly caught in honey. It dragged her into following a pattern inside herself, a pattern that laid shadows on the quiet green of her soul.

It was only Fenn's touch that drew her back. Returned, she still felt an unclean remnant of that darkness remaining deep within. She shivered and wanted a bath, but knew that soap and water couldn't cleanse her of what she was feeling. The stain lay too far inside.

"That," she began. "It's . . ."

Words failed her and she was unable to finish.

"Evil," Fenn said.

There was a stirring in the air, heralding the waking of Druswid, the spirit of the oak itself, at whose sufferance Fenn studied and lived in his branches. He did not manifest physically, but his presence was undeniable all the same.

It is a poison, the treewizard said.

Angharad shivered again. Slowly the green silence inside her was overwhelming the patchwork shadow that the box's design had laid on it. But the memory of its presence wasn't so easily forgotten.

"What is it?" Angharad asked.

On the surface, Druswid replied, *a simple puzzle-box. The kind any merchant's daughter might have on her windowsill to entrance her friends.*

"But that design . . ."

Angharad gave the scryer a quick sidelong glance, shifting her gaze away from the brass bowl almost before it touched the metal surface. She couldn't help but wonder—if its mere image was so powerful, what damage would its physical presence cause?

We called that design glascrow *in the old days,* Druswid told her. *The green death.*

Angharad thought of the ancient enmity between the Lords of Summer and Winter.

"Is it Lithun's doing?" she asked.

Its source is not the Winterlord, the treewizard replied, *for it causes havoc with his gifts as well. Its origin is more ancient still—predating the stoneworks, predating the rivalry of Anann's sons. Whatever the design's origin, the knowledge is lost in antiquity. I know only that all the* glascrow *were either destroyed or banished from the Isles—a very long time ago.*

"And this one?" Angharad asked.

"Is here," Fenn said. "In the Isles."

"Where?"

We don't know. Its image lies in the scryer like a fisherman's net, waiting to draw the unwary into considering its pattern.

Angharad glanced at Fenn. "Where does it take you?"

Into madness; into a death of the Summerborn silences within, and, if left unchecked, the green itself.

"It would have taken me," Fenn said, "if not for Druswid." Now it was his turn to shiver. "I can still feel its taint inside me."

"And you let me look at it?"

Angharad didn't even try to keep the anger from her voice. The impurity was still inside her, like a bad taste in the mouth that couldn't be washed away.

That was my doing—not the lad's.

"Why?"

How can you know evil's danger unless you experience a sliver of it?

"The same way you know enough to not jump from a cliff—because it's a stupid thing to do."

"I'm sorry," Fenn said. "I . . ."

She laid a hand on his shoulder. "It wasn't your fault."

She looked around the room, but though the treewizard's presence was palpable, there was no visual point of reference. It was hard to direct one's anger at an invisible presence.

I understand your anger, Druswid said, *but the experience was necessary. Left unchecked, the* glascrow *can undo what little wonder the world retains. It will spread—slowly at first, but more quickly as it feeds on the Summerblood of Hafarl's mortal kin.*

"I agree to the danger," Angharad said. "But . . . Broom and Heather! I can still feel that darkness inside me."

Good.

"Good? How can you call it good?"

Because you must take your memory of it into the green and let the advice you acquire there point our way.

"Why can't you go?" she asked the treewizard.

"I wanted to," Fenn said, "but—"

Neither the lad nor I are tinkers and harpers as well as Summerborn. We can see into the green. But you can open the door into its silence. With your music, tempered with your tinker's blood.

Angharad nodded in unwilling agreement. A traveler's touch on a harp's strings—it carried a music more in tune with the green than that of one bound to a single place.

Music and moon. And the ancient riddling stoneworks.

Tinker, harper and witch.

Triads.

Calling-on magic born of threes.

"When?" she asked.

Tonight.

* * *

A half-league from the Druswid Oak was a solitary long-stone known by travelers as Ballan's Broom. It stood on the crest of a low hill; four times Angharad's height, it was a tall graceful stonework from the riddling elder days when wonder had a stronger foothold in the world of men than it did now. Waves of the surrounding gorse sea lapped at its base. As Angharad approached, a fox lifted its head to watch her with his secret eyes, vanishing into the gorse with a lift of his bushy red tail before Angharad had a chance to call out to him.

Looking at the longstone, backlit by a low hanging half moon, she marveled, as she always did, at how much this stonework did look like the handle of a giant's broom stuck into the earth at the top of the hill. How the men of the ancient times had raised such a slender shaft of stone never ceased to awe her. But the answer to that riddle lay lost in history. And she had come for another purpose tonight, looking for the answer to another riddle.

She laid her cloak on the ground, her walking shoes and staff upon it. Barefoot in the couch grass, with the dirt cool beneath the soles of her feet, she looked up the long height of the stone, then turned her back to it. She sat, leaning against its rough grey surface, harp on her lap, the moonlit hills spread out before her until their low backs were swallowed by the trees of Avalarn.

Even, she thought, even without the gift of witch-sight, there was more beauty to be found in the world than could ever be snared in language or music. And with the sight . . .

Her witcheries let her look deep into the night, the moonlight as bright for her purposes as the sun was for those without her gift. She watched the bell heather and gorse accept the patterning breath of the wind. Moths flew close at hand; higher was a pipistrelle bat. She saw a polecat stalking a hare, the hare escaping. A short-eared owl went by, so close she could almost feel the draft of his wings.

She could have sat and watched all night, and been well content. But she had another purpose for being here tonight.

She shifted her harp to her knee. No need to test the trueness of its tuning—she had done so already before leaving the oak—but she did so again all the same. The spill of harp notes tumbled from her instrument, deep and resounding for all the harp's diminutive size. When she began a slow air, the music floated like quiet thoughts over the gorse sea.

She thought she heard the bell heather's rosy blossoms tinkling in response.

The night held its breath, listening.

The stone grew warm behind her back.

Moon and music.

And her witchery made three.

She played until the moon hung low, then played in the dawn. When morning grew from dawn's pink smudge on the eastern horizon, she finally laid her instrument on her lap. Her fingers held cramps in every joint, the calluses on her fingertips were soft and aching. Sighing, she set the harp on her cloak and stood, stretching the stiffness from her muscles. Disappointment lay like a heavy mantle on her shoulders, weighing her down.

The kowrie hadn't come.

The triad of moon, music and witchery hadn't worked its enchantment.

Hadn't drawn her into the green.

She looked across the moors, but her sight was turned inward, to the memory of the puzzle-box's pattern and the shadows it had left on her soul. Blemishes on her green. Like dry rot, hidden from sight, but eroding her witcheries all the same.

Was that what had kept the kowrie away?

Was there a kind of cold iron inside her now, an anathema to the poetry of the green?

Best not to think of it. Best to come back another night and try again.

She put on her shoes and cloak, shouldered her harp. Staff in hand, she set off to return to the Druswid Oak. The twilight of the dawn lay expectantly all about her, but where usually its magic invigorated her, this morning it merely brought home all the discomforts of spending a night on the moors.

It was under the shadows of Avalarn's first outriding trees, just out of sight of the oak, that a voice called out to her.

"Daughter."

She paused to see a tall slender woman standing there in between the trees. Her hair was red-gold—a blazing blend of fire and honey. She was barefoot in a leaf-green kirtle, with a dark green cloak overtop. Her features were veiled and thin, her skin browned. Blue-gold lights flickered in the depths of her eyes.

"I heard your music," the woman said.

"Who—"

The woman held a finger to her lips. "No need for names or what they can call to us."

Angharad's free hand went to her breast as though to hide the stain of the puzzle-box's shadow from the woman, but the stranger merely shook her head.

"You haven't lost the green," she said. "We all carry dark places inside us—the *glascrow* merely wakes those shadows, gives them life."

"I'm not . . ." Angharad began, but then she thought. Not what? Not a bad person? Perhaps. But had she never known anger? Never held unkind thoughts? The stranger's observation was valid. No one was innocent of darkness.

"Druswid," she said. "He had me look at it and now I can't get the memory of it out of me."

The woman nodded. She wore a tired smile—the kind a mother wears for her errant child.

"He can be an old fool at times," she said, "but he was right in doing so. You needed a taste of the heart of its darkness to understand it fully."

"That pattern . . ." Angharad said.

Again words failed her.

"Is foul," the woman agreed.

Angharad shivered, remembering. She drew a breath, realizing that she was accepting a grave responsibility as soon as she spoke her next words.

"What can be done about it?" she asked.

"Find it. Wake it. Banish it."

"How?"

"The finding I can tell you," the woman said. "It was brought to South Gwendellan on a merchant ship. The waking is simple as well—though dangerous to one with our blood. It needs the Summerblood to be kindled, you see, but it feeds on our green."

"Then why wake it?" Angharad asked.

"Because only then may it be banished."

"Can you help me?"

The woman shook her head. The sorrow in her eyes made Angharad want to weep.

"Not I—I am bound to my place in the green. As Druswid is to his oak. As his apprentice is to the yoke of his past. We are bound to our places as surely as housey-folk are bound to their hearths."

"I . . . I don't think I can do it alone."

"There are Summerborn in Gwendellan," the woman said. "Few, it's true, and weak in witchery, but you can find them if you look."

"And they will help?"

The woman sighed. "I don't know."

"It isn't an easy task you're setting me," Angharad said.

"It isn't set for you, daughter. You take it up or not by your own choice."

"And if I don't?"

"The puzzle-box will find its way into the hands of a Summerborn who, all unwittingly, will solve its riddle. The patterning on its six sides merely wakens the shadows we all carry within ourselves. When the box is opened, it will loose its true power."

Angharad nodded.

Glascrow.

The green death.

And wonder would finally die from the world—not because it was forgotten, but because of some ancient evil that no one truly understood.

"I'll do it," Angharad said softly.

The woman smiled her sad smile. "I thought you might."

"And you can't tell me how to banish it?"

"The *glascrow* predates my time in this world, daughter. I know only that we of the green may not handle it. Imagine one of the green given over to the darkness, abusing his or her wonders . . ."

Angharad gave a shudder. A kowrie with dark magics . . .

"Only one who carries both human blood and that of the Summerborn has a chance to escape the shadows."

"Why?"

"Because their humanity tempers their Summer-blood—like the many folds of steel in a tinker blade. Resistant and supple, but nigh unbreakable."

"So I must wake it . . ."

"And face it. And banish it. Daughter, if I knew more, I would tell you. If I could, I would do the task myself—or at least accompany you."

But she couldn't, Angharad thought. She looked back over the moors to where Ballan's Broom was now backlit by the dawn sky. Mysteries, she realized, had their own laws. No matter how marvelous they appeared to common folk, they still followed their own natural order. As a hound couldn't fly nor an apple tree blossom with roses, so those of the green had their own strictures that they must observe.

"I understand," she said, turning back to look at the woman.

No one stood there between the trees. There was only her own long shadow on the grass, cast by the rising sun behind her back.

"I understand," she repeated softly.

Luck, she thought she heard a voice whisper on the wind as she continued on to the Druswid Oak, but it might have been only her own need calling the word up from the places of the hidden green inside her.

It wasn't until she was at the foot of the oak that she realized who it must have been that had spoken with her.

Tarasen.

Hafarl's daughter.

She borrowed a horse from a tinker company she met in the hills. The horse brought her to Codswill, where she took ship across the Channel Sea, then up along the coast of Southern Gwendellan to where Cathal harbors on the Grey Sea. Standing on Cathal's docks, swaying until she regained her land-legs, she stared at the bustling streets of the town.

Somewhere on its cobbled streets, in the buildings that crowded elbow to elbow against each other, or in the stately mansions on High Hill, the puzzle-box was waiting for her. Shadows chittered in her green and she shivered with a chill, though the sun was high, the afternoon warm.

She adjusted the strap of her journeysack on one shoulder, her cloak rolled and tied to it like a bedroll, the strap of her harp on the other. She pulled her shawl tighter about her red hair. Then, staff in hand, she went looking for help.

For one with Hafarl's gift.

One who was Summerborn.

II

THE FEAR SHE saw in his eyes was all too familiar. mirrored the fear she herself had felt when she'd looke into Woodfrost's eyes that first time and saw that he bor the Summerlord's gift of witch-sight.

"My name's Angharad," she told him. "I mean yo no harm."

"I'm not like you."

"I know. But you could be."

She hunched down near him, her journeysack slap ping one thigh, her small harp the other. She leaned o her rowan staff, letting the witch-wood take the great part of her weight as she leaned closer to look at him.

He crouched in the alleyway, half-hidden in a nest refuse—close enough for her to touch, though he mig] as well have been as far from the bustling streets of Cath. behind her as northern Ardmeyn was from the Mull Isle some three hundred leagues to its south. Goodwives an merchants filled Cathal's streets, haggling over the ma ket wares; laughter and sharp words, and all the soun in between that men and women make when they ba gain, rose from the crowded stalls where they went abou their business. But he hid from the light and sound an movement, hid in the rubbish and debris with the look of a half-starved dog about him.

It was hard to tell his age, but guessing roughly, she put it at twice her own twenty-three summers. His brown hair was matted and dirty, his cheeks and chin bristly with several days' growth of beard. He wore rags and tatters, the clothing hanging loose on his gaunt frame. His eyes were hollowed and haunted—one a startling blue, the other a milky white—and his skin was grimed with dirt. He reeked of ale.

But it was still there inside him—the Summerblood.

And looking closer, Angharad could see that the dirt and rags and unkempt hair hid more than a lame leg and a blind eye. They hid what remained of a soldier. Wounded, no doubt, in the war that Gwendellan and Thurin had fought against the Saramand, across the Grey Sea. Wounded and left to fend for himself, now that Gwendellan's kings had withdrawn their armies from the strife.

He was a beggar, here in Cathal, but once he had marched in the regiments, as proud as any young soldier.

"What . . . what do you want from me?" he asked.

"I mean you no harm," Angharad repeated.

"No harm? Look at you! They've taken everything from me—are you here to take my soul as well?"

She understood his dismay. In her pleated skirt and white blouse, a grey shawl hiding the bright red of her hair, with the harp on her shoulder and staff of witchwood that she leaned on, it was plain to see what she was: tinker, harper and—if you knew how to spy the Summerblood—witch. Not a one of them was overloved, though it was the witchblood that could hurt her the most, were it discovered.

Housey-folk abided tinkers for their metalwork and mending gifts, and a harper could be counted on to provide music more exotic than a worn old fiddle or

squeezebox, so they were given a grudging welcome a
well. But witcheries. . . . Housey-folk had little patienc
with witches and *their* gifts.

If they only knew . . .

But knowing took the sight, to see beyond the worl
that is, to see into the green—Hafarl's realm, the Middl
Kingdom where the kowrie dwell except for those night
when the moon, or music, or both, call them forth t
dance in the old stoneworks that riddle the Green Isle:
Without the sight, housey-folk had only a harper's poetr
to describe those fading wonders, and practical a
housey-folk were, they believed only what they could
hold and weigh, not what they were told.

So she understood his fear, no matter the ignoranc
it was based upon, no matter that he had the gift of th
sight, locked away behind the anxiety that made him
tremble to look at her. She had worn that fear herself—
worn it like armor against the magics of those with th
blue-gold witchlight in their eyes.

She tried to disarm him with a smile.

"I haven't come to steal your soul," she said. "I'v
come to give it back to you."

Grimy fingers clutched at the rags covering his chest
"I . . . I never . . . lost it."

"Are you happy?" she asked him. "Are you content
Do you wear respect for yourself, even if others don't?"

The blue eye grew shiny with unshed tears. "Don't . .
just don't . . ."

Say any more, Angharad finished for him. Don't re
mind me of who I once was. Let me hide the memories in
the same ale-fog that hides my pain.

Her heart went out to him.

"I don't mean to hurt you," she said. "But if you
could *see* . . ."

"See what? That a dog, foraging on the streets, i
looked upon more fondly than one such as I?"

"You—"

"No, *you* listen."

The alcoholic haze lifted momentarily from his gaze; the dampness in his eye was shiny now with anger.

"They look at me and I remind them of the war we didn't win. I remind them of all those who *didn't* come back. They want nothing to do with me. And who can blame them? What have I to offer them? I've no learning. I've no strength to work the docks or farms. Tom Naghatty went overseas a boy, looking to become a man, but he came back only a half-blind, lamed beggar, worth nothing. An old sack filled with bad memories for whomever looks upon him and remembers."

Angharad slowly shook her head.

"That's not true," she said. "You could show them the green."

"The green," he said. "That's for children to see."

"It doesn't go away from you—you leave it behind."

Tom gave her an unhappy smile. "Easy for you to say, with your harp and your eyes. You reek of witcheries."

Angharad glanced nervously over her shoulder to the busy street behind her.

"I do?"

"Not to them—but to me. To any of us born with the curse."

"So you do remember."

"Much good it does me."

"But it doesn't have to be a curse," Angharad said. "I remember the first time I—"

"I don't want to hear any more. Go away. Leave me alone. You don't want me, you don't need me, and you won't have me."

Angharad nodded, as though agreeing with him, but she made no move. She remained hunched there in front of him, her weight still on her staff, her mild gaze steady on him. A strand of red hair had come loose from her shawl and she blew it away from her cheek.

"Woman," Tom said finally. "Why aren't you gone?"

"My name's Angharad," she said.

"I don't care if it's Tarasen, you'll still not have me. For what, I don't know, but better the troubles I know, than the worse ones the witchblood will lay on me."

"It's odd you should mention her," Angharad said.

"Who?" Tom asked. "Tarasen?"

The weariness was back in his voice. The alcoholic haze returning to his one good eye, dulling the blue like a smear of fog rising up from the sea in late afternoon.

Angharad nodded. "Hafarl's daughter. It's because of her that I'm here."

And then she spoke of the events that had brought her to Cathal.

"What do you *want* from me?" Tom asked her when she was done telling her tale.

If her words were seeds, Angharad realized, they had fallen on stony ground. Though he'd once been a soldier, he was one no more. The green that lay within him carried a blight at its core as surely, and as dark, as one born in the *glascrow*'s shadows, but this one was born of the horror of the battlefield. Now he was done with struggles—except for the struggle to eke out a drunkard's existence on the streets and back alleys of Cathal.

Perhaps he had earned the right to let others do the fighting now. Perhaps it was unfair of her to even ask.

"Woman," Tom began again.

"Angharad," she said absently.

"Angharad, then."

The blue eye was clear once more, the ale-fog held at bay. She heard an honest regret in his voice, but there was still no acquiescence in it.

"I can't help you," he said. "Neither the merchants nor those wealthy enough to live on the Hill take the time to gossip with an old drunkard lying in an alleyway. I can't begin to guess where you should look for this puzzle-box of yours. And I am tired. So very, very tired."

Angharad nodded. She reached over and grasped his grimy hand with her own.

It's true that you're weary, she thought at the startled look that crossed his features when she touched him. *Your youth worn away and wonder fled, but you aren't yet so divorced from the world that you can't still be surprised.*

"I understand," she told him. "It was unfair of me to ask."

This close to him, the reek of his body odor and alcohol was almost overpowering. She concentrated on what remained of the green within him—the Summerblood that had called her into the alleyway to find him nesting here in the refuse.

"You've already done your part in preserving the beauty of the world," she added.

He pulled his hand free of hers. "Don't mock me."

"I meant no mockery. You gave the strength and health of your youth and half your sight for your country. Had the Saramand ravaged our shores once more, much of the Isles' beauty would have disappeared. I honor you for that."

"I don't need your pity either."

"Nor my friendship?"

"Just go away."

Angharad rose to her feet with a sigh. "May I ask you one more question?"

His fingers tore at a scrap of discarded paper stained with grease, shredding it. His shoulders were as sloped as the rounded hills of Cermyn—not from age, as those old hills were, but rather from a hundred small defeats. He would not look up.

"What?" he said.

"Where can I find other Summerborn?"

The gaze of his one blue eye rose to meet hers. His face was turned so that she could not see the other, his profile that of a hawk or a falcon.

Once, she thought, he had been handsome. War and the street had stolen that from him as well.

"They're lost," he said. "Or drunk. Or hiding."

"Hiding? From what?"

"The witch-finders—what else? Do they love the Summerborn in your homeland?"

"All the Isles are my homeland."

"Well, *this* part of your homeland has fallen prey to witch-finders."

He seemed about to say more, hesitated, then finally looked down at the small heap of shredded paper by his feet. Angharad waited to see if he would say more.

"What do you mean?" she finally asked.

She knew there were those without the sight who feared the Summerborn and fought that fear by bringing harm to its source. And there were always men who would satisfy that need by bringing them the fingerbones of the Summerborn. One of the sailors on the ship on which she'd arrived in Cathal had been wearing a necklace of such bones.

"There is a man," Tom said, "who made his fortune following the lines of battle. He had goods that were needed that he would provide if you could meet his price. His men haunted the battlefields, robbing the dead. It was whispered that he even traded with the enemy when the fighting was at its worst. Now he lives on the Hill, his past forgotten by those who would rather not remember."

"What has he to do with these witch-finders?"

"It seems he has a use for those Summerborn."

"What use?"

Tom shrugged wearily.

"This man . . . what is his name?"

"Aron Corser."

A premonition stirred in Angharad, a shadow crossing her heart as chilly as those brought to her by the puzzle-box's pattern. She stored the name in her memory, for all that she wished she'd never heard it.

"Thank you, Tom," she said. "Go gentle."

Again, he looked up. "Go gentle," he repeated softly. "There was a story my mam used to tell me that always ended with those words."

"I know it," Angharad said. " 'Cony the Tinker.' It's a travelers' tale."

Tom nodded. "When the soldiers shot him down— the beekeeper's daughter spoke those words over his grave. I always remembered that story."

"I did, too. Because of its sadness." And later, she thought, for how it was twin to her own life—her own love lost, as senselessly slain as Cony was, though it was a plague that took her harp's namesake, not the work of men.

"Why is it that we always remember the sadness more?" she said, her voice soft.

"I didn't remember it for its sadness," Tom said. "I remembered it for the strength of their love."

The war had stolen more from him than his youth and health, Angharad realized. He'd left a girl behind and when he returned. . . . Had she rejected his broken body? Or had she already forgotten him before ever he returned?

It was the plot of a hundred ballads, but no less painful if the story was your own. Yet somehow he had remembered the good of what they'd had, rather than the loss.

The green silence inside him was less withered than he let on.

"I wish I could," she said.

"What?"

"Remember the love more than the sadness."

A bittersweet smile touched his grimy lips. "It's all I have," he said.

Angharad nodded. "Go gentle," she said again and turned away.

He called her back before she reached the mouth of the alley.

"Angharad."

She turned, not sure she could bear another of his sorrows. He might be able to forget them, but she could not. They were a part of her now. She took them willingly—for that was part of a poet's task—regretting only that in taking them, she did not lessen his burden.

"There's an inn on the south side of the market," Tom said. "The woman who owns it is a friend to those you seek, though she doesn't have the curse herself. You'll know it by the sign of the pipe and tabor above its door."

"Thank you, Tom."

"Be careful. The witch-finders know her as well. They watch her, marking her customers and friends."

"I'll be careful."

He nodded. "You do that."

He burrowed deeper into his nest of rubbish as she turned again. But that wasn't the image of him that she took away with her. She remembered instead a young man she'd never known. A young man who, no matter what he told himself or others, would never admit defeat.

12

PERSECUTION OF THE Summerborn was not a new custom, but it was a tradition perpetuated more on the Continent—in Sarama and the Hundred Kingdoms of Thurin—than in the kingdoms of the Green Isles. At this time in the Isles' history, it was a rarity, frowned upon by most because they didn't believe in witchery in the first place.

But there were always some who believed. Some who saw not wonder, but danger, in a Summerborn's eyes. Angharad had run across scattered pockets of them before, once barely escaping with her life. They could be found anywhere, but their numbers were strongest among those who lived on the shores nearest the Continent—Northern and Southern Gwendellan, and the northeast peninsula of Fairnland.

Angharad had kin on the Continent—the travelers had kin everywhere—and she had heard the tales. . . . But she had not heard rumors of a recent concentrated upsurge of enmity against the Summerborn in the Isles themselves. It wasn't until she saw the sailor with his necklace of fingerbones that she realized hard times were coming once more for those who bore Hafarl's gift.

At least they were coming for those foolish enough to remain in Gwendellan.

The fingerbones of the Summerborn were supposed to store their witcheries, bringing those who wore them a piece of a Summerborn's soul—the part that gave witches their luck and longevity. All one truly needed was one bone, from one finger, but when the wearing of such bones was in fashion, men and women took to wearing bracelets and necklaces, even dangling earrings, made from the fingers of many witches. The more one had, the greater the luck. The longer the life.

Or so the old tales said.

Unfortunately, Angharad knew the old tales to be true.

Witcheries did live in a Summerborn's fingers, in their fingerbones. It was a fingerbone that had given Fenn his second chance. It was fingers that woke the music that called forth the green. It was the movement of fingers, combined with the power of names, that let wizards work their spells. It was fingers that shaped the Sign of Horns that kept ill-luck at bay.

Fingerbones held the marrow that gave the Summerborn their witcheries, just as the sacred stone underlying the earth was Anann's witchery. The ancient stoneworks that riddled the Isles were *her* fingerbones.

Trade in such goods dealt mostly with ancient relics from Summerborn long gone into the Land of Shadows, or with the bones stolen from graves of the recently dead. It had been a long time since the Isles had known a terror time, a time when witch-hunters stole the bones from their living victims.

There were stories of fingerless Summerborn—alive, but with their witcheries stolen—who had wandered the countryside, shunned by all who came into contact with them. Unable to fend for themselves, they soon died—of hunger, for they could neither harvest nor hunt nor earn their way without the use of their hands; of the cold and frost when Lithun ruled and winter lay upon the land.

Many took their own lives.

Long ago.

Angharad remembered the sailor again.

Had his necklace consisted of relics or witcheries stolen from those already dead? Or had a new source for a Summerborn's fingerbones been found?

Were Aron Corser's witch-finders providing him with a supply of witcheries taken from the hands of living Summerborn?

Angharad flexed her own fingers and shivered.

Bad enough to lose their use, to never play her harp again, to be dependent on others simply to eat, to clean herself and dress—if others could be found willing to take on the task. But the loss of those witcheries would also close her off from the enchantment that her music could call up on those nights when the moon was right.

To have the sight but not its use.

Only a memory.

To lose the green.

I will be careful, Tom. As careful as careful can be. I will borrow the wariness of Tarasen's shyest charges—the hare, the deer—trusting not to my luck, but to caution.

For she could not abide it.

To lose the green.

The very thought made her feel sick and weak, when what she required now was strength.

From the small store of coins she had left, Angharad replaced her tinker garb with clothing more suitable to one of the housey-folk. When she finally approached the south side of the market, she wore the knee-length grey kirtle of a fisherwoman, with its sleeveless top and divided skirt; an embroidered blouse cut low in the bodice, following the local fashion; straw sandals and her old shawl to hide the blaze of her red-gold hair.

Not all Summerborn had red hair, but many did. In a place such as this, where most hair colors tended to drab browns and black, it was enough to set her apart. And that she could not afford. She needed to be invisible, rather than catch anyone's eye.

Her journeysack bulged with the addition of her tinker garb and her small harp. The instrument was stowed away since being a harper was also enough of a novelty to call attention to her. Besides, it was common knowledge that, while a harper wasn't necessarily Summerborn herself, she would know those who carried Hafarl's gift in their blood.

Through the poetry of their music, harpers could see into the green.

Witch-finders would be very interested in harpers.

Pendall Street marked the southern edge of the market. Beyond it were the narrow streets of Cathal's poor, where the housey-folk lived in close squalor, the buildings decrepit and crowding each other, the streets littered with refuse. Pendall itself was a wide busy avenue that ran from the Merchant Quarter to the docks, with a wide range of inns on either side of the street.

The Pipe & Tabor was on the poor side of the street, down by the docks, and Angharad had no trouble finding it. She stood across from it, a few doors down under the shadow of a sign with a foaming mug of ale, and regarded it for a long moment. She could see no one watching the place, but that meant nothing. The witch-finders could easily have taken a room in the inn behind her, or in any one of the others that were close enough to offer a view of the Pipe & Tabor.

She gave a nervous tug at her new clothing and

wished she were anywhere but here. But it was too late to turn back and she had nothing to gain by standing outside. It would only call attention to herself.

My name's Ann Netter, she reminded herself. I've come here from Mewer, on route to visit my cousin in Eynshorn who has work for me. No, I'm not a witch. Nor a tinker or a harper. Just myself—a fisherwoman.

She looked down at her hands.

A fisherwoman. With calluses on her fingertips—the tips of a witch's fingers, no less—and none where one would gain them from working the nets, or cleaning the day's catch, or the hundred other tasks that such a woman would have.

Still, they would just have to do.

She squared her shoulders, but before she could take a step, the door to the Pipe & Tabor opened with a bang as its thick wooden panels hit the stone wall of the inn behind it. Two men came out, holding between them a struggling boy of no more than fourteen summers.

The boy was a street urchin—reed-thin and hair all tousled. He had a lean hungry face that was smudged with dirt, and his clothes were such a ragged patchwork that Angharad couldn't tell where one garment left off and the other began.

Her sight told her that he was Summerborn.

She didn't need her witch-sight to tell her what his captors were. Witch-finders, the pair of them, and two of a kind with their stocky bodies, thick shoulders, groomed hair and the fine cut of their clothes. Prosperous witch-finders.

"Let me go, you stupid louts!" the boy was shouting. "If I was a witch, don't you think I'd've fried you both by now?"

The witch-finders didn't bother replying. They merely dragged him along the street where men and women stopped and looked, but lifted no hand to help the boy. Here and there, Angharad saw fingers shaping the Sign of Horns, warding the boy's ill-luck away from themselves.

Angharad took a step towards the struggling threesome, then stopped.

What was she doing? They were two to her one. She might be able to call up a witch-fire with her staff—enough to startle them—but that would merely be revealing her for what she was. And that would be no help to either the boy or herself.

Better to wait.

She knew where they were taking the boy. To Aron Corser's. She could plan first, then see about helping.

The witch-finders had dragged the boy almost to the end of Pendall now, where the street opened onto the docks. Looking at the scuffling threesome, thinking of the trapped boy, the fear she had seen in his eyes, Angharad flexed her fingers. She could almost feel the press of a cold iron blade against them, where finger joined hand.

The iron cutting through skin and muscle, popping the finger free from its end joint . . .

She took another step, but hesitated once more as a new thought came to her.

How could she have been so blind? Aron Corser might well be stealing fingerbones from living Summerborn—but that was only *after* he was done with them.

She thought of the *glascrow* and remembered Tarasen's words.

It needs the Summerborn to kindle it.

Aron Corser wanted a witch to solve the riddle of his puzzle-box.

It feeds on our green.

Why the merchant would want that, Angharad didn't know. She could see a profit in the selling of witches' fingerbones, but loosing the *glascrow* on the world, letting its shadow swallow the green. . . . There was no profit in it. It made no sense.

Unless he simply hated Summerborn.

Hated them enough to destroy the source of their gift.

Men were capable of any hate, any madness.

Swallowing thickly, she watched the witch-finders drag away the boy. When they were finally around the far corner, she crossed the road towards the inn.

She wasn't done yet—not with Aron Corser, nor his witch-finders. But first she needed to speak to the owner of the Pipe & Tabor. First she needed to find the Summerborn who had not yet been taken.

13

 $\mathbf{T}$ HE PIPE & TABOR was the oldest building on Pendall Street—one of the oldest in Cathal—dating back to a time when it had stood by itself at the edge of the original Old Market. The town had grown up around the inn and market, the common in front of the inn first becoming a dirt track, then a cobblestoned street that was now lined with the buildings of the Pipe & Tabor's finer and more prosperous cousins. But for all the gilt and finery of its competitors, the old inn had an air about it that put Angharad at her ease as soon as she crossed its threshold.

Its interior was clean, if shabby. It was obvious that whatever profit there was to be made in the inn went to stocking the kitchen and bar, rather than decoration. The floors were well-worn stone, strewn with straw and rushes, the walls paneled with oak, the hearth smoke-blackened fieldstone. The tables and chairs were of a plain older style—roughly hewn in comparison to present fashion, but eminently serviceable. Old cotton curtains were pulled back from the windows to allow illumination; wall sconces and smoke stains on the walls themselves showed where the candles were set at night.

Angharad stood for a moment while the door closed

behind her to let her eyes adjust to the light. It being mid-afternoon, there were few customers. A pair of old codgers, bewhiskered, the one with a pipe, the other chewing on a twig, were sitting at a table by the hearth playing drams. A stout, round-faced merchant with what appeared to be his son—the two were so alike—shared another table. A fifth man, his features hidden in shadow, sat by the window overlooking the harbor. A barmaid was polishing tankards by the bar.

Angharad looked at the girl. Tom had spoken of the owner as being a woman, but somehow she doubted that this slip of a girl was she. The door to the kitchen opened then and a tall, grey-haired dame stepped out into the common room, carrying a tray laden with sliced beef, fresh-baked bread and a tureen of soup which she brought to the merchant and his son.

Despite her grey hair, the woman couldn't have been much older than thirty summers. She had a pronounced overbite that gave her face a horsey cast; her figure was trim where it should be, and full elsewhere; her features were pleasant, her eyes warm, her smile infectious. When she glanced over at her, Angharad couldn't but be charmed by her.

"Welcome to the Pipe & Tabor," the woman said as she approached, wiping her hands on her apron. "My name's Edrie Doonan. How can I help you?"

"I'm . . . ah . . . Ann Netter," Angharad replied.

Edrie smiled, taking in the bundle of Angharad's journeysack and her fisherwoman gear.

"First time in a town so large?" she asked.

"No—I mean, yes. It's all so bewildering."

Edrie nodded. "Will you be wanting a room?"

"I . . . yes. Of course."

This was all going wrong, Angharad realized. She wasn't used to putting on a false face. The lies stuck in her throat. She had never before hid the fact of who and what she was.

A tinker, and proud of it.

A harper, and skilled at her trade.

A witch, and there was no shame in that either.

"Well, we have rooms in plenty," Edrie said. "Is there only the one of you?"

Angharad nodded. She cleared her throat.

"But it isn't just about a room that I've come," she said, pitching her voice lower.

Edrie's eyebrows rose quizzically.

"That boy," Angharad said. "The one those men were taking away . . ."

The warmth began to leak from the innkeeper's eyes. "What of him?"

"I've come about him as well," Angharad said. "I'm looking for those with . . . with the gift."

Like a cloud blocking the sun, the friendly warmth fled completely. Edrie regarded Angharad coldly now, her lips pulled tight and thin.

"Get out of here," she said.

"But—"

"Get out, or I'll have my stablehand throw you out."

"You don't understand. I'm here to help, not—"

"I won't repeat myself again, *Ann* Netter or whoever you really are. I want you out of my inn; if I could see it done, I'd have you out of Cathal and the Isles as well."

She stood very close and poked Angharad's shoulder with a stiff finger.

"Am I making myself clear?"

Angharad nodded numbly. "V-very clear," she said.

"Then why are you still here?"

"I'm not what you think I am," Angharad tried as she turned for the door.

"Your kind never are. There's worse things we can do

than barter a few coins for another's freedom, but what that might be, I can't think just now."

"But—"

"Out!"

Angharad had the door open by now. Edrie gave her a shove and Angharad stumbled out onto the cobblestones. The inn door slammed shut behind her.

For a long moment Angharad simply stood there, staring at its worn oak panels. She was frustrated and angry and half-inclined to set her rowan staff against the wood and set it aflame with a witch-fire, but common sense prevailed.

The innkeeper thought she was in league with the witch-finders—that she went ahead of them to point out likely candidates for capture in return for a few coins. Never mind that the woman was wrong, Edrie Doonan and she were still allies. The innkeeper simply didn't realize it yet.

Angharad looked down Pendall Street.

Now what? She still needed lodgings. She still needed to find other Summerborn to help her. The *glascrow* remained unfound and Aron Corser had captives that needed rescuing.

She was beginning to get a headache.

First, lodgings, she decided. She shifted the strap of her journeysack to a more comfortable position and was about to set off down the street to choose another inn, when the door behind her opened once more. Angharad turned, a hopeful smile on her face. But it wasn't Edrie, having reconsidered her treatment.

It was the man who'd been sitting by himself by the window.

Out here on the street she could see him better. He'd the brown Gwendellan hair and ruddy complexion of a man who worked either the sea or the land. His clothing was plain—serviceable gear, rather than fashionable—

and he had an honest face, with a twinkle in his eyes that
kept the smile on Angharad's face.

"I'm sorry," she said. "I thought you—"

"Were Edrie, come out to change her mind? Not
likely. Once she gets an idea, there's no shifting her."

Angharad nodded. "Yes, well . . ."

"Couldn't help but overhear the pair of you," the
man went on. "Talking about Jackin and all."

"Jackin?"

"Jackin Toss—the lad what the witch-finders
snatched."

"I was just . . . curious," Angharad said cautiously.
"That's all. I was wondering what he'd done."

The man shrugged. "Born with the wrong blood, is
what. Lad never had much luck. Grew up on the streets,
barely making do, and now this. Sets a man to wondering
what the world's coming to."

"Can't anyone stop them?" Angharad asked. "The
witch-finders, I mean."

"Who's to stop them? These parts, the folk don't
much care for those born with the witchblood in them.
Town guard turns a blind eye—so long as there's no trouble on the streets themselves. What the witch-finders do
with their catches when they get them home . . . well,
that's of no concern to the guard."

"But it's wrong."

The man nodded. "Course it is, but that's the way of
the world, lass. Everybody knows. You'll be a stranger,
I'm guessing."

"I'm from . . . Mewer," Angharad said, remembering
her story and forcing up the lie.

"I meant a stranger to Gwendellan."

"Oh, no. I've come here from Mewer—on my way to
Eynshorn to stay with my cousin."

The man nodded again. "Suit yourself. I'm Billy Perrin. I've a few acres west of Cathal, a stall in the market

that I work mornings. I've a lad working for me afternoons, but he's growing fatter than my purse is—if you get my meaning."

Angharad smiled. "He eats more than he sells."

"Exactly my problem. Now you're looking a bit twiggish your own self, but I'm thinking that even if you'd eat, you'd eat less than him."

He paused expectantly. Angharad simply looked at him.

"It's a roundabout way of telling you that if you could use work, I could use a worker."

"That's kind of you, but—"

Perrin held up his hand. "Don't care where you've run away from, or why—just so long's as you do your job, I'll be happy."

"I . . . I'll have to think about it," Angharad said.

Perrin nodded. "Don't think too long. The lad I've got'll be out on his ear before the week's up and I'll be needing *someone*. Might as well be you."

"Thank you. I will think about it."

"Stall's on Bendy's Lane—beside the butcher shop at the corner of Wheeker. I'm there mornings till noon. Afternoons I'm at the farm. You take the Old Road, straight out from the Merchant's Quarter, and it's a half-hour ride—longer afoot. We're at the end of the lane that starts at the burnt oak."

"Thank you," Angharad said again.

Perrin caught her arm before she could go. "A wee word of advice, Ann Netter. Don't be so curious of them that has the old blood in their veins. And don't be talking about what a shame it is no one helps them—no matter how you feel. The walls have ears, never doubt it. Even on the street."

"I'll remember."

"You do that." He motioned down the street with his

chin. "The Badnough Inn's cheap and not nearly so roguish as its name might let on."

He patted her arm, then tipping his hat, set off down Pendall, heading towards the Merchant's Quarter.

That was kind of him, Angharad thought. If only The Pipe & Tabor's owner could have been so friendly. But she understood Edrie's worry. If the innkeeper was a friend to the Summerborn, and they were being abducted from her inn . . .

Edrie was right in being suspicious of any who came along asking about those who bore Hafarl's gift.

Adjusting her journeysack's strap yet again—the extra weight was making her shoulder sore—Angharad gave The Pipe & Tabor a last wistful look, then set off herself, looking for the inn that Billy Perrin had recommended to her.

14

FROM A WINDOW of her common room, Edrie watched the woman and Farmer Perrin talking on the street outside her inn. The nerve of the woman, coming in bold as brass not ten minutes after her friends had dragged off Jackin.

Except . . .

The longer she watched the woman, the more she began to wonder. Bold as brass, this Ann Netter had been. That in itself was strange. Most of the witch-finder's whiddlers hid in the shadows, pointing out their prey and taking their blood coin without ever showing their faces.

Bold as brass . . .

Edrie went back over her conversation with the woman and realized that she'd been hearing only what she'd wanted to hear, not what was being said.

I'm not what you think I am.

I'm here to help . . .

As Perrin turned away and the woman started off down the street, Edrie glimpsed a lock of red-gold hair poking out from under the woman's shawl, there one moment, gone the next as the woman pushed it back under with a quick finger.

Red hair.

And that staff with its white wood . . . it had to be rowan.

Witch's wood.

Arn help the woman, Edrie thought.

I'm looking for those with the gift . . .

Ann Netter had to be Summerborn herself, come seeking her kind. She meant no harm indeed.

Edrie hurried to the door and stepped out onto the street, but by the time she was ready to call out after Ann Netter, the woman was already out of sight.

"Damn," Edrie muttered.

Bold as brass, indeed. Rather a born innocent, for it was as plain as the nose on Edrie's own face that the woman knew next to nothing of subterfuge. The whiddlers would spot her in a moment. And then the witchfinders would have her snatched and away before the day was out.

I've come to help.

She'd come to help, but all Edrie had done was send her to her doom.

She went around behind the inn to the stables calling for her stablehand.

"Owen! Shake a leg, lad."

The young man who came at her call was a gangly lad—all long limbs and slender torso. His head was topped with a thatch of brown hair that inevitably had enough straw in it to make a stork's nest. He cleaned his hands on his trousers as he approached Edrie, curiosity plain in his dark brown eyes.

"Yes, ma'am?" he asked.

"I've got a job for you," Edrie told him.

"A job?"

The innkeeper smiled. "One you'll like. It involves gadding about in the streets after a young woman."

"Ma'am?"

"Come along," she said, "and I'll tell you all about it."

15

EDRIE DOONAN WAS not alone in watching the conversation between Angharad and Farmer Perrin outside the Pipe & Tabor that afternoon. Across the street, standing at a second-story window in the Gallant Archer, a tall man with dark grey eyes watched as well. He was neither whiddler nor witch-finder, but he had an interest in the Summerborn all the same.

"Lammond?" a voice called from inside the room.

"A minute," he replied, never taking his gaze from the scene below.

He had watched the witch-finders take away the boy from the inn across the street and been about to turn away when he spied the fisherwoman approaching the same building. There was something in the way she moved that tickled a memory at the back of his mind, but she had disappeared inside before it could surface. He'd been still standing there, trying to call it up, when the door of the Pipe & Tabor opened again, the innkeeper bodily ejecting the woman from her establishment.

Curious.

And still that tug of memory.

He'd studied the woman, the set of her head, the

trimness of her figure in her fisherwoman's garb, the bulging journeysack, the staff. Fisherfolk rarely traveled far, so it was odd to see one so obviously burdened down for a long journey. She didn't have a fisherwoman's walk nor her demeanor either. It wasn't something he could quite place, but if pressed, he would have said that her movements were too lithe, her bearing too imperturbable.

And there was that nagging memory, like a lost word sitting on the tip of his tongue, but hopelessly unremembered.

He watched her conversation with the farmer, watched them part.

"That woman," he said more to himself.

"Which one?"

His companion had left the bed where she'd been sitting to come stand beside him at the window. Lammond glanced at her.

Even in her shift, without her rouge and paints, there was no mistaking Veda Purdon for anything but what she was—a high-priced courtesan with a sense of style that was all her own. Contradictions abounded in her. She was elegant and yet earthy, refined and yet bawdy, slender and yet voluptuous . . . in short, whatever a man wanted her to be, so long as he could afford to pay her fee.

"That fisherwoman," Lammond said. "With the pack and staff."

The woman he indicated had a stride that was long and loose—the stride of one used to the open road, rather than ships and harborfronts.

"I see her," Veda said. "What about her?"

"She reminds me of someone . . . or something."

Veda laughed softly. "It's her staff."

Her staff. Of course. How could he have been so blind?

White witch-wood.

"She's Summerborn," he said.

And a fool, for all her clever disguise. Did she think no one knew of the bond between rowan wood and witches?

Veda nodded. "The one role I can't play."

"Why would you want to?"

A sly smile stole across her lips. "Let me tell you about the men who live on the Hill," she said. "I know a half-dozen who'd pay as much as most folk make in a year for one night with a witch." She cocked an eye. "It has something to do with their fire," she added. "Or is it with their fingers?"

Lammond made no reply.

"Apparently they can keep a man poised on the brink of consummating their passion for hours."

"Spare me."

The fisherwoman was out of sight now, but Lammond had marked her. He had a hunter's eye. He would remember her no matter where he saw her again—even if only from the rear. He knew her step, the set of her head, the lift of her shoulder.

"But then you'd know all about witches, wouldn't you?" Veda teased.

"I know enough," he replied.

He turned from the window and fetched his jacket from where it hung by the door.

"Will I see you tonight?"

"I thought you were working."

"I am—but only until midnight. You know Master Beman. He's in and out and asleep within a half hour."

"But you'll stay to give him his money's worth."

"We're the same in that regard," Veda said. "Professionals."

Lammond smiled. "That we are."

The door closed softly behind him.

16

Taking Farmer Perrin's advice, Angharad rented a room in The Badnough Inn. It was around the corner from the Pipe & Tabor, directly on the docks. From the customers in its common room, Angharad assumed that it did a regular business with sailors and fisherfolk.

She'd had better lodgings.

With her rapidly dwindling resources, and no time in which to earn more, all she could afford was a small closet of a room, up on the third floor near the servants' stairwell. There was space for a narrow bed and a chair by the window overlooking the roof of the inn's stable out back, but little else. A ceramic bowl for washing and a pitcher filled with lukewarm water sat on the windowsill; a brass chamberpot was under the bed, sweet-smelling herbs sprinkled in it.

It wasn't the sort of room that could tempt Angharad into spending a great deal of time in it. Leaving her journeysack on the bed, she started for the door, then looked at the staff she was still holding.

Now this was wise, wasn't it just?

After all her care at hiding what she was from the

Cathalians, she'd been marching through their streets with a staff of white witch-wood in hand.

But without the rowan wood, she felt too un-protected—especially with witch-finders about. The staff did little more than call up fire, but it also had an aura about it that, if nothing else, made her feel more confident.

She leaned the staff against the wall and sat down on the bed, dragging her journeysack near. She took out a leather bag rolled up in an old tunic. The bag was filled with small folded paper squares of various medicinal powders and bundles of dried herbs. It also held her fetishes and charms—though few housey-folk would recognize the items as such.

At the bottom of the bag was a small bundle of rowan twigs tied together with a bit of twine, which she removed and put in the pocket of her skirt. Stowing the herb bag back in her journeysack, she rose once more.

The twig bundle, while far less tangible than her staff, was still rowan. It still made her feel better having its weight in her pocket, the aura of its witcheries enclosing her with a protective warmth.

Moments later, she was slipping down the servants' stairs and out the back door of the Badnough. Dressed as she was, no one gave her a second glance.

Her invisibility proved a blessing until she reached the bottom of High Hill. The streets widened here and were overhung with the boughs of old oaks and elms. The houses were set well back from the street as they rose up towards the Hill, nested in green swaths of well-trimmed lawns and gardens. Low stone walls separated the grounds from the street, where the only traffic appeared to be carriages and the well-dressed wealthy, strolling in couples and threesomes.

The street names alone spoke of wealth and privacy. The Lord's Walk. Bellsilver Lane. Peacock Avenue.

On the Hill her fisherwoman's garb would draw attention to her as surely as the moon and music drew kowrie from the green.

But she had to go up the Hill all the same.

Her current run of luck had not been auspicious. She'd been in Cathal for not even a day, but already Tom Naghatty, the only Summerborn she'd been able to find so far, was unwilling to help; Edrie Doonan saw her as one of the foe; and there were witch-finders and their whiddlers scouring the streets for those with Hafarl's gift. It didn't take a great deal of consideration to realize that the only Summerborn she was assured of finding and who would both want her help *and* hopefully help her in return were those held captive by Aron Corser.

So she had no choice. She had to rescue them from his place on the Hill.

Where she couldn't go, dressed as she was. And she didn't have the coin to purchase yet another set of clothing—especially not at the prices she would have to pay for the styles that were worn by the well-bred women on the Hill.

She would have to wait for night, she thought, frustrated at yet another delay.

But then a serving girl walked by her, a wicker basket over her arm that was laden with fresh vegetables and pastries. The smell of the pastries made Angharad's stomach rumble. She watched as the girl walked the length of a block and then turned up a back lane. The girl must work in one of the houses on the Hill . . .

Of course, Angharad realized. The folk of the Hill wouldn't want their servants traipsing about on the street, in plain view of their neighbors. They would have private lanes behind their houses—for the servants, for the carriages and horses to be stabled.

A fisherwoman wouldn't be out of place walking there. If she was asked, she could always say that she was looking for work.

Please, ma'am. I'll work ever so hard.

Smiling, Angharad gave the servant girl a good lead, then followed her up the lane. She'd asked one of the stablehands whom she'd met behind the Badnough for directions before she'd left. Now she counted off the backs of the houses, hoping she could find the place as easily from the rear as the stablehand had told her she would find it from the street.

There was only one way to find out.

17

FIND AND FOLLOW a fisherwoman.

Owen's mistress had given him odd tasks before, but this easily ranked among the oddest.

"Her name's Ann Netter," Edrie had said. "Mark where she's lodging. See where she goes and who she talks to, but don't speak to her yourself."

And what would he say to her if he did? Your pardon, ma'am, but my mistress has sent me out skulking in your shadow. Do just go about your business and pay me no never mind?

"And if there's any news," Edrie had finished, "bring it to me quickly."

"What sort of news?" he'd asked, but that had just earned him a sharp poke in the shoulder from her finger.

Well, he had news now, yes he did.

Where Pendall met the docks, he'd nabbed himself a Lowtown boy—Johnny Tow, who claimed to be one of the Upright Man's lieutenants.

The Upright Man ran a string of pickpockets and petty thieves out of Lowtown, though he didn't live in the poor side of Cathal himself. No one knew his name, and no one ever saw him except for Hogg the Catcher, who handed out orders and collected the profits, so it was easy to claim whatever one wanted in terms of one's place in the thieves' hierarchy. What was more telling, perhaps, was that Tow was allowed to continue with his boasting. No one doubted that if Tow wasn't what he said he was, the Upright Man would soon set matters straight in a manner that would be most unpleasant for the boy.

But while the Upright Man's identity was a mystery, if one spent any amount of time on Cathal's streets, one quickly learned how to spot the raggedy street urchins who worked for him.

Like most of his peers, Tow was thin and wiry, nimble and quickfingered, with a mouth on him that would put a sailor to shame. The promise of a penny—to be collected from Edrie at Tow's convenience—garnered Owen the information that, yes, he'd seen the fisherwoman with the fat pack and white staff. She'd gone into The Badnough not twenty minutes past, and, blood of a virgin, wasn't that her now, stepping lightly from out of the stableyard behind the inn?

Owen turned to look, marking the woman's shawl and garb.

"What's up then?" Tow wanted to know.

Owen shrugged. "Don't know. Got a message for her from the mistress, that's all."

Tow gave him a considering look and Owen could see the cogs whirling in the boy's mind as Tow thought of how he could put this business to more profit for himself.

"You've already earned a penny," he told Tow. "Best leave it at that—unless you want Edrie coming after you with a broom."

Tow laughed. "Better catch your scaly-girl quick, then," he said, "or she'll be leaving you behind with your head up your arse and nothing but the broom to look forward to yourself when you get home."

Owen nodded. The woman had a long stride and was rapidly getting away from him. A moment later and she'd be lost in the crowds. He started after her.

"Two pennies, you said?" Tow tried, catching his arm.

"Argue it with Edrie," Owen replied.

He shook off the boy's grip, checked his pocket to make sure his own small moneybag was still there, and hurried off after his quarry. The fisherwoman was no longer in sight.

"Maybe I will," Tow said.

Owen had to smile. Not likely. Edrie had a heart as big as the harbor, but little patience for the likes of Tow when he was trawling for coins. A bargain was a bargain, so she'd pay the penny, but both Tow and he knew that she'd never pay two. She knew as well as anyone what such a little piece of news was worth.

"And maybe I won't!" Tow called after him.

Owen trotted up the street until he had the fisherwoman in view once more, then held to the pace she kept.

Find and follow the fisherwoman.

Well, that was proving easy enough.

See where she goes . . .

Owen had a sinking feeling as he followed the woman across the market. Sure enough. She was heading for the Hill. Now how was he supposed to follow her up there? If the town guard caught him prowling about the Hill's hoity-toity streets, they'd take him for one of the Upright Man's urchins.

Mind you, he thought, dressed as she was, Edrie's fisherwoman wouldn't be going very far either without being stopped.

He got close to her as she paused on Bellsilver Lane, right there at the foot of the Hill, and relaxed when he saw the indecision on her face. Good. She realized she wasn't garbed for this place as well. But then she spied a serving girl. She gave the girl a considering look, then after waiting a moment, followed her up one of the back lanes that went up by the rear of the stately houses.

Sighing, Owen followed.

Was there ever a lad taken on at a hiring fair that got a stablehand's job such as his? He spent as much time gadding about the town on one errand or other as he did in the stables themselves. Not that the Pipe & Tabor did such a booming trade with those rich enough to keep horse, but still there was work enough to . . .

He came to an abrupt halt and darted in behind some hawthorn bushes. Not a half dozen feet in front of him, while he was busy complaining away to himself, the fisherwoman had paused. A hoyer—one of those shaggy tan and-grey dogs that had been brought to the Isles from the Continent since the end of the last war—had come out of a nearby yard to growl at her.

Don't try to make friends, Owen thought. A hoyer will as soon bite your hand as lick it.

But the fisherwoman showed no fear. She knelt on the grass verge of the lane and held her hand out to the dog. Hackles lifted about its neck, the dog approached her on stiff legs. Owen wanted to turn away—he hated the sight of blood—but he felt as though he was frozen in place.

"You're a long way from home, aren't you?" the fisherwoman said.

The hoyer gave a few short barks, but they didn't sound threatening. More . . . quizzical, Owen thought, beginning to feel confused himself. The beast's hackles were lowering and it began to wag its tail.

"No," the woman said. "But I have kin there."

Something odd happened whenever she spoke. Owen heard a buzzing in his ears—a low, humming undercurrent that echoed in unison with her words.

The dog barked again.

"Yes," the woman said. "I'm looking for kin here as well. Their blood sleeps, but they are still in great danger because of it."

Again the hoyer barked.

"I thought you might have seen them. Does he keep them in the house?"

A low growl came in response.

"I could. But where would you go? If you're seen with me, they'll merely bring you back and throw me in their gaol."

A whine.

"All right. I'll come back for all of you tonight."

She acted, Owen thought, as though she was conversing with the dog. He imagined himself telling Edrie about this.

Do I have news for you, mistress? Indeed, I do. Your fisherwoman's stark raving mad. For today's lark she went creeping about the back lanes of the Hill, talking to animals. Fair gave me the creeps, it did.

Though what was eerier still, he realized, was that he could almost imagine that the hoyer was talking back. That they understood each other.

He began to circle about the hawthorn bush he was hiding behind, so that the fisherwoman wouldn't see him when she turned to go back to the market.

Careful now, he told himself. If she talks to animals, maybe she talks to bushes too.

He had just got himself better hid when he heard the crunch of boots against the dirt surface of the lane. Looking out through a webwork of branches and leaves, he saw Aron Corser's two witch-finders approaching the woman and the dog.

Witch-finders.

The woman talking to the dog.

Arn help him, he'd been shadowing a witch.

Owen started to feel a little sick.

18

"YOU'RE A LONG way from the harbor for a scaly-girl."

So intent had Angharad been on her conversation with the hoyer that she hadn't noticed the approach of the two men. When she did look up to find them regarding her, her pulse quickened uncomfortably.

Of all the bad luck. They were two of Corser's witch-finders—she recognized them immediately. The same two who had taken the boy, Jackin Toss, away from the Pipe & Tabor earlier that day. Now here they stood, swaggeringly tall and broad-shouldered, hands on the hilts of their swords, their attention all too plainly centered on her. How much had they seen? How much had they heard?

She hid her sudden dismay behind a quick nervous smile and rose to her feet.

"Looking for prawns, were you?" the other man asked.

"Oh no, sir. I'm—"

"In deep trouble, skulking about where you don't belong," the first man said. "Perhaps you'd like to explain to the guard what you're up to?"

Beside Angharad, the hoyer bristled at the man's sharp tones. A low growl rumbled in its chest.

Don't, she willed to the dog. You'll just make it worse.

Unfortunately, for all the small gifts that her Summerblood gave her, speaking mind to mind was not one of them. As the hoyer took a stiff-legged step towards the men, she reached into her pocket for her bundle of rowan twigs. A face full of burning twigs probably wouldn't stop them, but it might be just enough for her to make her escape.

"Back off, Magger," one of the men told it.

As the hoyer hesitated, the man gave Angharad a suspicious look.

"Curious," he said. "It's not like the hound to take so to a stranger, is it, Dagor?"

"Not normal at all," Dagor agreed.

"Makes a man wonder if there's more to this scaly-girl than she'd like us to believe."

Dagor took a step closer, ignoring the hoyer's warning growl. "Doesn't have the fish reek about her, either, Hoth."

Angharad gripped her rowan bundle more tightly. Ballan damn them, they weren't giving her much choice.

"Might be she has some kind of . . . magic about her," Hoth said.

Witch-finders. They had a kind of sorcerous talent as well, but it wasn't one granted by the Summerlord. They were Lithun's unwitting agents, gifted by the Winterlord with the ability to bend men's wills to their own. And to smell out witches.

She might have stayed hidden from them if she'd been able to stay out of their way, but at such close proximity as this it was impossible for her to hide her Summerblood from them. They knew what she was, as surely as tinkerfolk recognized their own, no matter where they met. She could see it in the men's eyes. Now they were merely toying with her for their own amusement.

"Talking to the hound, wasn't she?" Dagor said.

Hoth nodded. "Sure sign of a witch—conversing with animals."

"Turned old Magger against us, while here we are, doing his master's work for him."

"Doesn't seem right," Hoth agreed.

Angharad noted that Magger's threatening growls appeared to make no difference to them. With what she'd heard of the hoyer breed, she knew that the dog could take a man down more quickly than most men could unsheathe a sword. And since it was obvious that Magger was determined to protect her, the witch-finders were either a pair of fools or very good at the warrior's trade.

Given their relaxed stances, the easy assurance with which they carried their every movement, Angharad feared it was the latter.

"Best you call off the dog, witch," Dagor told her. "Master Corser won't be too pleased with us if we have to kill his prize hoyer, but he'll understand the why of it when we tell him the whole of the tale."

"And then it's you he won't be pleased with," Hoth said.

Dagor nodded. "You don't want to even consider what that will be like."

"I've no magical alibi—" Angharad began.

"Cram it sideways, witch," Hoth said, the mildness of his voice belying the intent of what he said.

Dagor nodded. "Or we'll do it for you with the butt of a sword—*after* we kill the dog. Master Corser collects your kind, but he doesn't much care what shape they're in when we bring them to him."

"There's only one part of you that he requires intact," Hoth said.

Dagor smiled. "And I believe you know what part my brother means."

Angharad shivered slightly, fingers trembling out of sight in her pockets. The knuckles of the hand holding the rowan twigs were white from the pressure she exerted on the bundle.

To call off the hoyer was to admit to what she was. But she didn't see that she had any other choice. The witch-finders couldn't be so calm unless they were capable of killing Magger. She didn't want to be responsible for the poor creature's death. But to just give herself up to them . . .

She started to take her hand from her pocket, calling up the witch-fire from the rowan as she did.

A new voice stopped her before she had the bundle free and ignited.

"Are you having some trouble with these men, miss?"

Neither she nor the witch-finders, not even the hoyer, had heard the stranger approach. One moment they were alone in their confrontation, the next he was standing nearby, a tall man with handsome features and dark grey eyes. Not a lord nor merchant from the Hill, but not a commoner either. Angharad couldn't place him at all. There was a sense of hidden power about him, but it had neither the taste of Lithun's touch nor the green.

"This doesn't concern you, Lammond," Hoth said.

Angharad was surprised at the uneasiness that now touched the witch-finder's voice.

"Let me decide what concerns me or not," the stranger said. He turned to Angharad. "Are they bothering you?"

Keep it simple, she told herself, for there's far more at play here than meets the eye.

She nodded in response to his question. "I was just

looking at the lords' houses, sir," she said. "I stopped to pat the dog—I . . . I had a dog at home—and then these men began their bullying . . ."

"That's not surprising with the brothers Staiyon."

"I've just never seen houses so fine," Angharad said, putting a proper touch of wonder to her voice.

The stranger nodded, then turned his attention to the Staiyons. "She's under my protection now—understood?"

"Corser won't like—" Dagor began.

"Ask me, do I care?"

Hoth held up his hands in a placating manner. "This round belongs to you, Lammond, but it doesn't end here."

"I have the time," the stranger said, "if you care to finish it now."

Hoth shook his head. "I don't think so." He gave his brother a sharp look, then turned his gaze to Angharad. "Think you're rescued, do you? You'll be wishing you came with us before this is through."

He turned his back on them and set off down the lane. Dagor hesitated for a long moment, then turned as well to follow his brother. The stranger waited until they were well away before finally turning to Angharad.

"Lammond d'es Teillion, miss," he said. "At your service."

Angharad returned his short bow with an awkward curtsy. "Ann Netter, sir. Thank you ever so much for helping me just now. I don't know what I would have done if you hadn't come along. They were saying the most awful things."

Easy, she told herself. Don't lay it on too thick.

She regarded Lammond from under lowered eyelashes, trying to read him. What was the source of enmity between him and the witch-finders? Had she finally found herself an ally—

Think you're rescued, do you? the witch-finder had said.

—or had she merely stepped from an obvious danger into a more subtle one?

The short time she'd already spent in Cathal had left her thoughts so knotted up that she wasn't ready to trust anyone.

"The Hill's not the place to go strolling," Lammond said. "Not unless you're one of them."

He said that final word with distaste.

"Oh, I see that now, sir," Angharad said.

"Call me Lammond—I'm no lord."

"If you please, Lammond, sir."

He shook his head, but didn't correct her a second time.

"I never meant to cause any trouble," Angharad went on.

"I never thought you did. Do you have a place to stay in town?"

"I've a room at the Badnough Inn."

"Let me walk you there," Lammond said.

"Oh, thank you."

Angharad had to hide a smile at the look of exasperation that came into her rescuer's features. Good, she thought. I'll play up the ingenue, if that's what it takes to keep a distance between us.

She bent down and ruffled Magger's fur. "I'll be back," she breathed in his ear, then stood up.

"Goodbye, pup," she said aloud.

Lammond shook his head. "Pup! Did you know that on the Continent they train those hounds for the battlefield?"

"Mor!" Angharad said. A fisherfolk's exclamation. "Have you *been* to the Continent, sir? I mean, Lammond. That is . . ."

She called up a blush and cast her gaze down at her feet.

"Come," he said. He took her arm and led her back down the Hill. "I'll tell you what it's like in those lands across the Grey Sea."

19

TOM NAGHATTY COULDN'T get the witch to leave his head.

He lay in his nest of refuse in the alleyway where Angharad had left him, face turned to the alley's dead-end wall, but he was blind to its stonework. Instead, he saw only her. She sat there behind his eyes, endlessly stirring his memories; her features so heartstoppingly reminiscent of another face, from another time, a time lost long ago; that damnable kind look in her eyes, the sweet tone of her voice . . .

"Damn the woman."

He rolled over to look out the mouth of the alleyway where the townfolk bustled about their business in the marketplace. He sat up slowly. For the first time in months he was aware of how he smelled—a foul combination of rank body odors, stale beer and Dath knew what else. He looked down at the grime under his nails, the dirt worked into the pores of his skin, the rags that passed for clothing.

He worked hard to forget. The times he wasn't drunk, or sleeping off a drunk, he was acquiring the wherewithal to get drunk. It was a simple, mindless existence that he had developed to a methodical perfection. It didn't require the interference of a witch to undo with a few kind words. That kindness woke memories best left where they belonged—with his missing eye and the full use of his leg.

The witch wanted him to feel again, but feeling encompassed remembering, and remembering only hurt. What use was the gift of the green if all it brought was pain?

"Damn her."

He stumbled to his feet, gaze blurring. It took him a moment of leaning against the wall, a time of shallow breathing while he waited for the sick feeling in his gut to subside, before he felt well enough to shuffle down to the mouth of the alleyway. A hand thrust into his pocket told him that he had enough coin for one flagon of ale.

One flagon.

It wasn't enough, but it would have to do until he could beg the price of a proper forgetting.

About to step from the alleyway, he paused.

There she was again.

The memories churned inside him, raw and bleeding. And Dath help her, but wasn't she in the company of d'es Teillion himself?

Someone should warn her, he thought. He could do it. All it would take was for him to call out to her over the crowd. But that would bring d'es Teillion's attention to him. He couldn't face those dark grey eyes. Not again. He could remember all too clearly having that tall lean frame, with its perfect posture, bent over him, the long narrow sword held negligently in one hand, the sword tip toying with the rags on his chest while d'es Teillion said, "Tell me a story . . ."

Memories.

That was what they all wanted of him.

Memories.

Warning that damnable woman would do the same thing. In her gratitude, wouldn't she redouble her efforts to help him? And wouldn't that just make him remember all the more?

But he didn't want to remember. All he wanted to do was to forget.

So he watched the two figures, her trim form set side by side with his more predatory height, the pair of them strolling the market like old friends, her hand tucked into the crook of his arm. He watched until the crowd swallowed them from his sight.

Then he went to drown his memories in that flagon of ale.

One flagon.

It wouldn't be enough.

It was never enough.

20

EDRIE LISTENED TO Owen's stumbling account of what he had seen, her concern growing proportionately as the story unfolded.

"What house was it that she stopped at?" she asked when he was done.

"The witch-finders spoke of Master Corser—and there was the hoyer, wasn't there?—so it must have been his house."

Of course, Edrie thought. The hoyer. Who else in Cathal had one of those vicious hounds? And where else would a Summerborn go to help her kin but to the lair of the creature who collected her people?

"You said she spoke to the hoyer?" Edrie asked.

Owen nodded. "It was—" He shaped the Sign of Horns with a quick nervous action of his fingers. "It was like she wasn't talking *to* it, ma'am, but *with* it. Like they understood each other, if you know what I mean."

"With it," Edrie repeated softly. Her voice was distant, her gaze distant.

"Is she a witch, ma'am?"

Edrie blinked. "A witch? I don't think so. No more than Jackin's a witch."

There. That wasn't a complete lie, was it? Let Owen make of it what he would.

Her stablehand nodded slowly. "But then why did the witch-finders want her?"

"Who knows? She's pretty, isn't she?"

Owen grinned. "Very."

"No doubt they were trying to scare some favors from her."

"Oh."

And then they'd turn her over to their master, who'd cut the fingers from her hands to sell the bones . . .

She thought of young Jackin, trapped there in that house, with those men. She thought of them taking *his* fingers. Jackin was a pint-sized scoundrel, an unabashedly unrepentant rogue who tried her patience too far, too often; but he didn't deserve such a fate. He needed help—as others, also taken by Corser's men, had needed it before him. Perhaps, with this young witch at her side, she could finally do something to help those who survived.

And avenge those who hadn't.

"And it was Lammond who rescued her?" she asked finally.

"Yes, ma'am."

Lammond d'es Teillion. An enigma. Little was known of him and even less rumored—and that was odd in a town that thrived on gossip. But the guard was wary of him, as were the Lowtown brigands, from the Upright Man's urchins to Tave Maspic's people. And that in itself spoke volumes. There was only one piece of hearsay that tracked him like his shadow: few who captured his interest survived.

It wasn't a fixed specific, but it was the only bit of gossip that was repeated often enough that, to Edrie's thinking, it had to have some basis in truth. And if it were true, then Ann Netter might well be in as much danger at this

moment as she would have been had Corser's men suc-
ceeded in kidnapping her.

The girl needed to be told. And she was owed an apol-
ogy as well for the way Edrie had treated her earlier
today. If Edrie hadn't sent her off as she had, the girl
might never have run into either the witch-finders or d'es
Teillion.

Edrie rose from the kitchen table where they were sitting and fetched her shawl. "Tell Shanni I'll be out for
awhile. I won't be long."

She was out the back door and gone before Owen
could ask where she was going.

21

VEDA WAS IN her room when Lammond returned to the Gallant Archer. She sat at the mirror, regarding her reflection. Spread out on the table in front of her was a collection of powders, rouges and the like.

"Back early?" Lammond asked.

Veda shook her head. "Haven't been out yet."

He nodded bemusedly. Taking off his sword, he hung it by the door, then pulled an armchair over to the window. Elbows on the arms of the chair, chin propped in his cupped hands, he looked out the window.

Veda turned from the mirror. "So," she said. "What's she like—this witch of yours?"

"Strong."

"Is she the one?"

"She could be."

"What have you done with her—or should I even ask?"

"I haven't done a thing. I walked her to her room in the Badnough and came back here."

Veda hesitated for a long moment.

"That's not like you," she said finally.

Lammond turned his attention away from the window to look at her. A half-smile touched his lips.

"Jealous?" he asked.

"Hardly. But I am curious."

Lammond nodded. "So am I. Why is she here? What does she want with Aron Corser? She's hardly a professional, what with her half-hearted, albeit honest, attempts at subterfuge."

"What do you mean?"

"Think about it. Her disguise wouldn't hold water for a moment. The story she tells—"his voice changed to a breathy, high-pitched mimicry of Angharad playing the innocent fisherwoman"—my name's Ann Netter, sir, and I'm off to live with my cousin in Eynshorn who has work for me."

Lammond laughed. "Ann Netter," he said in his own voice. "Can you think of a more obvious false name for someone pretending to be a simple fishergirl? She hasn't a callus on her hands—except for the tips of her fingers."

"I don't understand," Veda said.

"That's the sign of a harper, my sweet."

Veda nodded in understanding. "I see. At least I think I do."

"Not only that," Lammond went on, "but I'll wager she's a tinker in the bargain. Think of it—harper, tinker and Summerborn, all tidily offered up in one neat package."

"Magical threes," Veda said.

"Exactly."

"So what do you plan to do with her?"

"Watch her for a day or two. Then we'll see."

Veda shot an involuntary glance to his leather journeybag where it lay in the corner of the room.

"Do you think she's been sent?"

"Undoubtedly. Corser's been none too subtle in what's he's about. What piques my curiosity more is, if

she has been sent, who sent her? And is she really as innocent as she seems?"

Veda smiled. "Why don't you simply charm her? An
hour or two of bed-play with you and she'll tell you anything."

"You overstate my talents."

"Hardly. I simply know that you had an expert
teacher."

Lammond laughed. "Get out of here," he said, "or
we'll have Beman's manservant pounding on the door in
search of you."

Veda nodded and went back to her preparations. She
paused at the door as she was about to leave.

"You'll be careful?" she asked.

He turned to give her a smile. "Always, my sweet."

When the door shut behind her, he looked out the
window once more. His gaze traveled to unseen distances
as he remembered every characteristic and nuance of
"Ann Netter."

Harper, tinker, witch.

How often did the fates offer up such a threefold
promise?

Not often enough to ignore the gift of it. Not often
enough at all.

22

ANGHARAD SAT ON the narrow bed in her room at the Badnough, holding her harp against her chest. A short fat candle burned on the windowsill, throwing shadows about the room. She ran her fingers along the length of the harp's strings and the smooth curve of its neck, yearning to wake its music, but afraid that by doing so she would call still more unwanted attention to herself.

So she sat in silence, merely holding her instrument, but it was hard to leave the green-born music that echoed inside her unsung. She could feel it stirring inside her, straining for release. The weight of the small harp on her lap, the feel of its neck against her cheek, was small comfort in the silence.

The whole of the day had gone badly. Playing the ingenue with Lammond. . . . She was beginning to feel that she hadn't been so much playacting as taking on the role in earnest. Broom and heather! She'd gone about everything in a backhanded manner.

Surely she was a more capable woman than the day had proved her to be?

Sighing, she laid the harp aside and leaned back

against the wall, hugging her legs to her chest, chin on her knees. A sense of dislocation had settled in her and she knew the exact moment that it had come upon her: when she'd looked into Fenn's scryer and seen the puzzle-box.

She could call up its damnable pattern so easily . . .

Too easily.

The shadow of it stretched deep inside her, a bewildering knot of dark aching that discolored everything she put her hand to, that had her stumbling through the day like a half-wit, unable to control the simplest situation.

Glascrow.

The green death.

Burrowed deep inside her, it had gathered to itself all the shadows of her soul and made a lair of them in which it now nested. And like the image of the box in Fenn's scryer, it wouldn't go away.

The green death.

It would be the death of her as well, she realized. Simply viewing it in the scryer was killing her, piece by piece, making a barrenness of the green reaches inside her. And when she held it in her hand? When she woke it, as Tarasen had told her she must to banish it, when she faced its power first-hand?

She started at the sudden rapping on her door, half-glad of the interruption, but apprehensive as well. With the way this day had gone so far, it was probably the guard come to shift her from the town limits because of her tinker blood. They were probably the only folk in Cathal that she hadn't quarreled with so far.

She stuffed her harp back in her journeybag and pushed the bag under the bed. Hiding her hair under a scarf, she took up her staff and went to the door. She paused before it to call up a witch-fire from the green inside her, keeping it easily accessible so that it would require no more than a moment's thought to set its white wood blazing.

Only then did she open the door.

She was prepared for anything—anything but the raggedy street urchin who stood there in the hall, grinning up at her from his dirt-streaked face.

"Yes . . . ?" she asked, feeling foolish to be standing there with the staff in her hand.

The urchin touched a finger to his brow. "Johnny Tow, ma'am. At your service."

"I'm not sure I understand."

"No need to play cagey with me, ma'am," he said. "Plain talk's needed here, I'm thinking. I've come to help you."

"Help me with what?"

Tow gave a meaningful glance over his shoulder and down the hall behind him before turning back to regard her again.

"Best we talk inside," he said.

Angharad merely looked at him. When he tried to sidle into the room, she blocked his way.

"I'm beginning to lose my patience," she told him.

Tow nodded. "Fair enough. We'll talk here in the hall then—only don't you be crying to me if word gets out and about town as to what we're up to." He dropped his voice to a stage whisper. "Even the bloody walls have ears—begging your pardon, ma'am."

"*We're* not up to anything," Angharad told him.

"Don't be so quick to—"

Angharad started to close the door.

"Wait!" Tow said. "One word explains all."

Angharad hesitated, then gave him a nod. "And what would be that word?"

Tow gave another look over his shoulder. Only when he was satisfied that they were still alone did he lean closer to her.

"Summerborn," he whispered.

Ballan, Angharad thought. Does the whole town already know me for what I am?

But she didn't let her alarm show. She *would* be in control.

"What about them?" she asked.

"I know you want to help them. Don't know why, but there it is."

"And you?"

"I'm here to help you."

Angharad gave him a long slow look and then nodded to herself.

"For a price, I'm guessing," she said.

Tow shrugged. "To cover expenses—nothing more."

Angharad shook her head. "I don't think so."

"I know a way into Corser's place—a secret way unguarded by his men or his hoyer."

"What makes you think I care?"

Tow sighed. "Your secret's safe with me. Ask anyone on the street—Johnny Tow's a man of his word."

Johnny Tow, Angharad thought, was barely out of his swaddling clothes. He couldn't be more than twelve years old. Hardly a man. But Angharad knew enough of his kind—she'd seen them in a hundred towns and cities—to know that whatever else he might be, and never mind his youth, he'd be cunning and capable of anything.

Street urchins bypassed their childhood. They grew up quicker on the streets through sheer necessity.

"There's another reason I'm here," he added, fidgeting under her calm gaze.

Angharad's brows lifted quizzically.

"This time they took one of my own."

"You mean Jackin?"

Tow nodded. "He's a mate of mine. It's not right what they've done—taking him like that."

"Even if he's a witch?"

"Jackin's no witch."

"Corser's witch-finders might argue with you about that."

Tow sneered. "They get paid by the head. If there's no witches around that everyone can agree to, they'll make one of their own."

"Wouldn't Corser find them out?"

"If Corser could sniff out a witch, why would he pay the Staiyons to do it for him?"

Angharad nodded. "But when his customers find out that the"—she hesitated over the word, only just suppressing a shiver—"bones are counterfeit?"

Tow laughed. "Do tell! Don't tell me you really believe there's such things as witches?"

"If there's no such thing as witches, then why collect their fingerbones?"

Tow shook his head as though she were simpleminded. "Doesn't matter if there is or isn't, folk'll still pay for the charms."

It was an unfortunate truth, Angharad realized. If there truly were no witches, only this belief in their fingerbones, there would still always be men like Aron Corser willing to deal in their supposedly magical charms.

But there were witches. And the charms did have power.

Angharad regarded the urchin for a long moment, weighing the earnest look in his features against his probable acting ability. He was, she decided, a far better actor than she, but an actor all the same.

"I'll ask you just one more time," she said. "What makes you think I care? What made you come to me?"

"Well, I've watched you, haven't I? Heard what you bought in the market—no scaly-girl, you, but you wear the clothes well. Seen you spying out Corser's place. Saw

Lammond rescue you from the witch-finders—have you known him long?''

"No. I only met him the once. Why do you ask?"

"Best be careful around him. He's a dangerous sort—easygoing, but there's a meanness in him that's easy to miss until it turns on you."

"We weren't talking about Lammond," Angharad said, "but about why you've come to me."

"That's true. Well, like I said—haven't I been watching you? It doesn't take much by way of brains to make sense of it all. You've come here in secret—come to rescue witches."

Angharad shook her head. "Somehow the logic of that escapes me."

She felt as she had many years ago when she first met Fenn and tried to convince him that she wasn't the tree-wife he'd decided she was. No matter what she told this Johnny Tow, he was bound and determined that he knew her mind. Unfortunately, unlike that time with Fenn, Tow had ferreted out the truth.

Broom and Heather! Was she really that apparent?

"You want payment from me to rescue your own friend?" she said at last.

"Just for expenses. I'd pay it myself, but I'm skint."

"What kind of expenses?"

"To hire a few Lowtown boys to cause a disturbance in front of the house while we slip in the back and out again with our prize."

To her surprise, Angharad found herself actually considering the boy's offer. One way or another, she had to get into Corser's house tonight. Why not take the help?

Because, a more reasonable part of her mind replied, it's as plain as the dirt on his face that he's not to be trusted for a moment. He means to make a profit from you, one way or another. He's as likely to turn you over to the witch-finders and collect a whiddler's fee as he is to help you.

Yes, Angharad thought. But forewarned is forearmed. He'll not take me by surprise.

"Ma'am?" Tow prompted her.

"All right," Angharad said.

She considered bringing her harp, but left it where it was hidden. Fetching her shawl, she tossed it over her shoulders.

"Lead on," she said, ushering Tow from the doorway and into the hall.

"You won't regret this," Tow assured her. "What a team we'll make."

Angharad closed the door behind them and faced him, staff in hand. "I'd better not regret it."

A surprised expression settled in his eyes at the grim set to her voice, an uncertainty that was there one moment, then gone again as though it had never been. He gave her another of his quick grins.

"I'll need a half dozen silvers," he said, holding out his hand.

"I'll pay your Lowtown boys myself when the time comes to pay," Angharad said.

Tow shrugged. "Fair enough."

He set off down the hall, humming under his breath, hands jammed in the pockets of his tattered trousers.

Angharad wished she felt better about the whole affair as she trailed along behind him, but it seemed too late to back out now. Not so much because of what Johnny Tow would think of her, but for what she'd think of herself. Having barely muddled through the day, she was determined to salvage something tangible, even if it meant boxing Tow's ears to get it.

23

THERE WAS NO answer when Edrie knocked at Ann Netter's door. She tried the knob, found that the door was unlatched, and let herself in.

The room was empty.

Sighing, Edrie stepped inside, closing the door behind her.

The damn fool of a girl. Where had she got herself to *now*? If she was out with that Lammond . . .

Better not to think too much about it.

Edrie quickly surveyed the narrow room. A cloak hung by the door, but there were no other personal belongings. And that was odd. Why would the girl have taken all but her cloak with her when she went out? That bag of hers had looked too heavy to be readily carted about.

She knelt on the floor to look under the bed and found the journeybag hidden there. Hesitating for a long moment, she finally drew it out. Undoing its leather ties, she pulled the bag open.

The harp came out first. It was a small instrument, beautifully crafted for all the plainness of its lines. She touched a string and was startled at the clarity and strength of the one pure note she woke.

Witch *and* harper. It grew worse by the moment.

Quickly she damped the string and went back to the bag.

Next she drew out a bundle of clothes and slowly unfolded the garments. Pleated skirt and a white blouse. A huntsman's leather jerkin.

Edrie had no difficulty in recognizing the distinctive style of the clothes. Tinker garb.

Arn love her. The girl was one of the traveling people as well.

A memory tickled at the back of Edrie's mind, there, but was gone again as soon as she reached for it. She let her thoughts quieten, considered nothing, and up it came.

She remembered.

A tale told round a fire. A tale of old magics, told by red-haired Summerborn. And Edrie was there. Paeter sitting beside her, his hand in hers, the firelight flickering on their faces and casting shadows across the farmyard to where their guests sat. The Grey Sea murmuring close at hand, down below the cliffs on which the farmhouse perched like a nesting seabird.

"In the old days," one of the Summerborn said, "it was different. The Summerblood ran thicker than it does in those few blessed with its gift today."

And Edrie had squeezed her husband's hand, for Paeter had the Summerblood in him, Hafarl's gift. It made him gentle, though strong. A poet, though he tilled the earth. It drew guests such as the three red-haired Summerborn who visited this evening, stopping at night before they traveled on.

"Today we are all that's left of the old magic," the tale-teller went on. "Our small echo of the gift us well apart from those around us. But in the old days, when the Blood ran strong, there was yet a deeper magic still— held by those who knew the calling-on magic, born of threes. Tinker, harper and witch. Moon, music and the stoneworks of old.

"Triads."

Looking at the clothing she held, Edrie remembered. Triads.

Like the woman whose room this was.

Tinker, harper and witch.

Did she know the old calling-on magic, born of threes? Could she wake the green and use its strength to put an end to that horror on the Hill? Aron Corser with his spiderweb of power that let him do as he willed, to whom he willed.

Tears glistened in Edrie's eyes.

For that old memory brought back more than the tale told by a red-haired Summerborn. It brought back the features of a man who died because he carried a sacred gift in his soul that set him apart from his fellows. A man set upon by his once-friends who'd been fanned into a witch-hunting fury by an itinerant priest. A man hung from a tall oak tree, his fingers broken and burned while he spun slowly from the hemp rope.

Paeter. Her husband.

Edrie wiped her eyes on her sleeve and returned the clothing and harp to the journeybag, the bag to its place under the bed. She stood and stepped quickly to the door, the room still blurry in her sight. The door swung open easily, but she paused before going through, wiping her eyes a second time before she looked about the small tired room.

She could have helped her, Edrie thought. She could have guested Ann Netter like a queen.

Instead she'd sent the girl off, alone into danger. Arn! Where to begin to look for her? She could be anywhere.

Edrie stepped into the hall. As she began to close the door, she paused as a smudged handprint on the doorjamb caught her gaze. A child's handprint. An urchin's dirt.

And she remembered.

How Johnny Tow had come by the inn that afternoon, looking for the penny promised him by Owen. A penny's worth of information concerning a fishergirl.

Had Tow come back to see what profit he could make from the girl himself? Led her off with his Lowtown lies, no doubt. Delivering her to the Upright Man for Arn knew what purpose . . .

She shut the door quickly and started down the hall, only to find her way blocked by a tall rakish figure. Lammond d'es Teillion himself.

"Edrie Doonan," he said. "What a pleasure. It appears we have a mutual friend."

He made a quick half-bow as he spoke. Edrie gave him a careful once-over, trying to decide if he were mocking her or not, then shrugged.

"Maybe we do," she said. "If she lives out the night."

"What do you mean?" Lammond demanded, his grey eyes darkening.

"I've a feeling the Upright Man's got her."

"I think not. What would he want with a simple fishergirl?"

Maybe, Edrie thought; more's to the point, what do you want with her?

"Well, if he doesn't have her now," she said, "he soon will. Her room's empty and I've a fair idea that Johnny Tow's been by to see her. What does that tell you?"

Lammond said nothing for a long moment, then he nodded.

"Come," he said.

Turning abruptly, he started off down the hall, not even looking to see if Edrie followed.

Edrie regarded his receding back.

Did she really want to get caught up any deeper in this? But then she thought of Ann Netter's innocent face, of how she herself had as much as tossed the poor girl out on the street.

Sighing, she hurried after Lammond.

24

JOHNNY TOW COULD barely contain his self-satisfaction as he led the woman through the back streets and alleys of Lowtown. There was a skip to his step, a smirk only just kept from his lips.

His one fear, going to the woman's room, had been that she was in tight with Lammond. No one—at least no one with their wits about them—crossed d'es Teillion. The best defense around him was not to be noticed at all. But since Lammond's rescue of the woman had been a chance encounter, as Tow had guessed from watching the pair of them at the time, he now knew that there was nothing to interfere with what he had planned for her.

"Is it much further?" the woman asked as one narrow twisting street led endlessly into another.

"Can't be too careful," Tow told her.

"That's not what I asked you."

Oh, do give it a rest, he thought. You'll get yours quick enough.

"Not far at all," he assured her.

"It had better not be."

He gave her a quick glance. The annoyance was plain in her voice and it didn't surprise him. What he did find odd, though, was how she retained her confidence where another woman would have been at least somewhat fearful by now, what with having been taken so deeply into Lowtown with no one but an urchin to show her the way out again. And then there was how easily she maneuvered her way by his side. The lighting was poor. The route he took her by was deliberately bewildering. He knew Lowtown as he did the back of his hand, but even he stumbled from time to time over some new bit of refuse.

The woman never once missed a step.

She had, he realized, the eyes of a cat. There was a feline grace to her stride as well, and a silence to her every movement that he was beginning to find unnerving.

Best see to business. Best see to it now.

He led her into a dead-end alleyway.

"This goes nowhere," she said.

How could she bloody tell?

"I know," he said. "This is where we'll meet them."

He put fingers to his lips and blew a shrill whistle.

"You trust these friends of yours?" she asked.

"With my life." Because they knew what was good for them.

"Even when they require payment for a favor?"

Tow shrugged. "There's risks. And they need to eat."

"Business been slow, then?"

"Business?" What was she driving at?

"Do you think I don't know a thief when I meet him?"

Tow blinked. "Think you're so bloody clever, do you? Then why'd you follow me down here?"

Now it was her turn to shrug. "On the off-chance that you *could* help." Her cat's eyes studied him in the dark. "I think it's best we go our own ways now."

There came movement at the mouth of the alleyway.

One by one, a near dozen street urchins moved into place, blocking the exit. There were both boys and girls in their number, each of them as raggedly dressed as Tow.

"A little late for second thoughts now," Tow said smugly.

The woman remained calm. "I'll be fair," she said. "Leave me now and there'll be no harm done."

Tow laughed. "No harm? Who gets hurt here tonight is up to us, you silly cow."

He reached under his tattered coat, a knife filling his fist when he brought his hand out again. The other urchins brought out their own knives and cudgels.

"We'll have our payment now," Tow told her.

"With the job undone?"

"Don't make things worse for yourself," Tow said.

Dath, was she a half-wit? They were seven to her one. True, she had a staff, but she couldn't defend herself from all sides at once, no matter how good she was with it.

"Put your staff down and give us your coin," he said. "All of it. Who knows? Do as you're told and we might even let you go unharmed."

One of the other urchins tittered at that.

Tow grinned. "It'd be a pity to have that pretty face cut up," he added.

"I think not."

Tow nodded to his companions and they moved in closer, brandishing their weapons until they had her boxed in at the dead end of the alley. They faced her in a half circle.

"Last chance," Tow said. "Put the staff down."

She merely regarded him with those cat's eyes.

"Silly cow," Tow murmured, shaking his head. He glanced up at the roof above them. "Do it, Chaffer."

Johnny Tow was no fool. He'd ordered one of his boys

o get up on the roof as soon as he had the woman in
place—all the threatening chat was just to give Chaffer
ime to get himself in place.

Why cut the woman when, pretty as she was, she could
bring a handsome price if delivered all in one piece? He
hadn't yet decided who to sell her to—Aron Corser, perhaps. Or the owner of one of the hussyhalls over on Akkers Street that catered to too rough a trade to be able to
hire their girls.

Before the woman could make a move, Chaffer
leaned over the edge of the roof and dropped a weighted
net on top of her. She went down, trapped by the net.
She still held her staff, though what good she thought it
would do her now with her limbs all tangled with netting,
Tow couldn't begin to guess.

He stepped over to where she lay and hunched down,
sitting on his ankles, so that he could look her in the face.

"What do you think now?" he asked.

Her cat's eyes glared at him. Poor silly cow, he
thought. But then he realized that she was smiling.

And her staff began to glow with a flickering witchlight.

25

THE BELL & HOGG stood at the corner of Akkers Street and Marner, a run-down excuse for an inn that catered to the rough trade from the nearby docks and those Lowtowners that could scrape together the price of a pint. The building was as shabby as its clientele; the interior worse than the weatherbeaten walls outside. There were mounds of refuse piled up against the stonework that was permanently stained a dark yellow from those beyond caring, or too drunk, to make their way to the latrines in back of the inn.

The inn was owned by a merchant who lived up on the Hill, but it was run by Boesan Cark, a barrel-chested man with a peg leg who had little patience with his customers in the first place, and less when their purses were empty.

With his head on a battered tabletop, his one good eye focused blearily on a pool of bile left behind on the floor by a patron even drunker than himself, Tom never knew Cark was coming for him until the innkeeper grabbed a handful of his greasy hair and gave it a pull. Tom's head lifted from the table, jerked upward like a marionette on a string.

"That's enough for you," Cark told him.

Tom tried to focus on the man's flat features, one hand scrabbling in his pocket for another coin. But the pocket was as empty as his life.

"No . . . no credit . . . ?" he asked, slurring his words.

Credit from Cark. That was a joke.

Cark's only reply was to raise the hand holding Tom's hair, lifting him from his seat.

The man just didn't understand, Tom realized. He couldn't see that old Tom needed to forget.

Kind eyes.

Features too similar to old hurts.

The green . . .

When Cark had him on his feet, he grabbed Tom by the back of the trousers with his free hand and propelled him towards the door, through it, out onto the street. There Cark released his grip with a final hard shove that sent Tom reeling, arms pinwheeling, his lame leg dragging him down. He fell in a pile of trash, thick with the stink of stale urine and rotting food.

"Come back when you can pay," Cark said.

He bore no grudges and cared not a whit for charity. Those that had coin could stay; those without were sent off until they could pay.

Tom watched a blurry double image of the innkeeper return to his commonroom. He tried to rise twice, but failed both times. Finally he simply lay there in the refuse, staring upward where stars hung in the night sky. He turned his face away when he realized what he was looking at.

Cark didn't understand. He needed the drink to forget. And he needed to be indoors at night. Otherwise the stars spoke to him. Sighing and whispering. Softly enjoining. Calling up the green from inside him . . .

He stirred when he heard that sound he feared the most.

It came from some great distance—from within himself, perhaps, or from some unimaginable faraway, it mattered not. Its source was that realm where the kowrie danced and enchantment bloomed green and wonder lay thick as the buzz of bees.

The green.

Called up in the belling of a stag.

Always the stag.

Its tines ringed with a gold nimbus. Its flanks red as a chestnut. Its eyes the dark of deep forests, green and dreaming. The moon reflected there. And wisdom. And mystery.

Forcing him to remember.

When he was a man.

A whole man.

When pain was a distant thing.

And memories were warm.

Tom dragged himself to his feet. Hands clapped against his ears, he bumped his way along the wall, his lame leg dragging along behind him.

But the belling of the stag merely grew closer. There was no hiding from that sound for, like memories, its place of origin was in that part of himself that he drank to forget, but could not.

"Damn her," he said, his eye shiny with tears.

Damn her for not allowing him to forget.

26

ANGHARAD DERIVED A certain sense of satisfaction from Johnny Tow's reaction to the blossoming of her witch-fire. His skin went ashy pale under its film of dirt. His eyes opened comically wide.

"Holy Mother of Dath," he said in a hoarse whisper.

Involuntarily, his fingers began to shape the Sign of Horns between them.

"You asked me," she said, "what do I think now?"

Behind him she could make out the reactions of the other street urchins through the webbed netting that entangled her limbs, her nightsight so sharp and clear that she could read every nuance of their fear as the witch-fire woke from her staff.

White rowan. Witch-wood.

In the old days, when the Summerborn were closer to the green, when the green itself was stronger, rowan could call up a witch-fire that would have consumed them all—each raggedy urchin, tattered clothes, grimy skin and all—and propelled their spirits into the Land of Shadows with the force of a storm's wind. But the years had taken their toll. The borders of the Middle Kingdom had steadily folded in upon themselves, receding from

the lands and memories of men; the green lost its potency. Now the witch-fire was far less powerful—merely a
pale echo of what it had once been.

But it could still burn easily enough through the rope
netting so that she could free herself of its entangling
folds.

It could still cast the illusion of great power.

Angharad rose to her feet, the witch-fire crackling all
about her. The urchins remained frozen where they
stood around her.

"What I think," she said, directing her words to Tow,
"is that you were too quick to dismiss witcheries."

She let the fire flare about her arms and shoulders,
arcing into a mantle of flames. When she pointed a finger at Tow, he broke and ran, his companions hard on
his heels. Moments later, Angharad stood alone in the
alleyway.

So, she thought, surveying her surroundings. And
what did this gain her? Wasted hours following Johnny
Tow about Lowtown. A rumor to run the length and
breadth of Cathal, fueled by fearful urchins, that there
was a true witch abroad. The Summerborn still to rescue
from Corser. The *glascrow* still to find . . .

Her witch-fire died down, returning to the wood of
her staff, from the staff back into the green. With its retreat came a sudden awareness. A shiver ran up Angharad's spine as she realized what she could have done.

Sweet Mother Arn. She would have killed them.

If the witch-fire still had its potency, she would have
simply burned them all away.

They were scarcely innocents, but they were still children. They were *people* and had as much right to this
world as any. Yet, had she been able, she would have
treated them with the same finality that mankind treated
the Summerborn. As it was, she had delighted in their
fear . . .

She leaned heavily on her staff and closed her eyes. And again the source of that new bloodthirstiness made itself evident.

In her mind's eye she saw the pattern of the *glascrow*, writhing like a self-sentient shadow in her mind, feeding on her darker thoughts. A poison in her spirit. A corruption discoloring her green.

Once more she called up the witch-fire, but this time she turned it inward, against the memory of the *glascrow*, against the hateful snakes that it had set writhing through her soul. Within her, the witch-fire still retained its potency, but the snakes fought hard against its scalding fire. In the end, she couldn't defeat them.

The witch-fire reduced them to a tiny pinprick of darkness that she secreted deep inside her, a small core of nightmare against which, she realized, she must constantly stand guard.

She could hide it away.

But she must never forget it was there.

She was slow to raise her head and study her surroundings once more. It took her a long moment to regain her bearings. Her staff was warm to her grip. Her head ached with a weary pain.

No time to rest, she told herself. She must do what she had set out to do or, for Jackin at least, it might be too late.

The Summerborn were her kin. No more of them would suffer—either the horrors that Aron Corser had in store for them, or the worse terror that the *glascrow* waited to loose on the green.

Sighing, she set off for the Hill, her nightsight and memory allowing her to navigate her way back through the labyrinth of Lowtown's twisting streets with the sureness of a native. The Lowtowners kept out of her way, thieves and drunkards alike. From time to time she caught glimpses of street urchins, grimy faces turning quickly away when she looked in their direction, but she didn't pause to pursue them.

Her business with Lowtown was done for the night— or so she thought.

She paused near the mouth of an alleyway and looked down its dark length. Her witchy nightsight pierced the gloom to see what her spirit had already sensed. She walked the few steps it took to reach Tom Naghatty's new nest and stood there, biting at her lower lip, as she looked down at him.

He twitched in his drunken sleep. Listening carefully, she could hear what he heard—the belling of a stag, distant and distant, but as close as thought.

As close as the green that they both carried within.

But unlike Tom, she had no fear of the stags that made the Middle Kingdom their home.

"If you could only accept," she began, her voice wistful, but then she shook her head.

Only he could work the change. Others could guide him, but only he could decide what he accepted to himself, and what he kept at arm's reach.

She went down on one knee and laid her hand on his brow, soothing him with a wordless song hummed quietly under her breath, until his limbs were still, his features peaceful.

"The green could give you more," she said. "The green could give you it all."

There was no response from the sleeping man, but she hadn't expected any.

Rising from his side, she left the alley to continue on her way, but a few blocks later was brought to a second halt by yet another odd sight: Lammond d'es Teillion and the innkeeper of the Pipe & Tabor, walking side by side ahead of her on the street.

What were they doing here? How did they come to know each other? Cathal was a small enough town, that was true, but Edrie Doonan and Lammond seemed to her to be too different from each other to be ever anything but chance companions. Yet here they were, obviously upon a shared errand. In Lowtown. Where honesty was an accident, rather than the norm.

She was quick to remember how Lammond had rescued her from the witch-finders, but she also remembered the fear in Johnny Tow's voice when he spoke of the man. That fear had been genuine—as had been Tow's warning.

There's a meanness in him that's easy to miss until it turns on you.

The witch-finders had been afraid of him as well.

A meanness in him.

Had she sensed even an inkling of it while she'd been in his company?

No, she'd been too busy playing the role of the breathless naïf to do much more than make note of Lammond's basic attributes. He was handsome. He carried himself with confidence and grace. He had rescued her . . .

Angharad's confidence in her own judgment had played itself false too often today as it was. Better to be suspicious of all and later pleasantly surprised at a mistake, she decided, than take the chance of falling into yet one more predicament from which, this time, perhaps neither luck nor her own abilities could rescue her.

So she kept to the shadows and gave them a good lead. When they finally turned off the street, she hurried up to the corner and waited there for a few moments before dashing across to the other side. A quick glance down the street showed that the pair were already out of sight, then Angharad was past the corner and making for the Hill once more.

They might have been able to help her.

Might have.

But it was best she did what needed doing on her own.

She could do it. Druswid and Fenn had confidence in her. So did Tarasen, Hafarl's own daughter.

She only wished she could borrow a portion of that confidence from them to carry inside herself.

27

AN HOUR OF walking Lowtown's streets, an hour of sidestepping refuse, fly-encrusted objects, sleeping drunkards, and Arn knew what else, had fairly much taken Edrie to her limit. All that kept her at Lammond's side was his single-minded purpose. He strode fearlessly through the darkest alleyway, caring not a fig for what he got on those polished boots of his.

Edrie was damned if she'd give it up before he did.

Once he stopped, head cocked as though listening. She paused at his side, the query dying in her throat when he touched her arm and shook his head. He looked back along the street they had just traveled up, then sighed.

"I thought I heard something," he said finally.

Edrie merely shook her head. What wasn't there to hear? Rats crawling in the garbage. Infants howling. Men and women arguing. Tomcats fighting. Drunkards attempting song. A pack of children racing by, one block over, trailing their shrieking laughter behind them.

It was late evening, though you wouldn't know it from the lack of quiet that held Lowtown's streets.

"What kind of something?" she asked.

"Footsteps—trailing us."

Lovely.

"Well, perhaps we should—" she began.

"This way," Lammond said, taking them down another side street, paying no attention to what she said.

Why had he even wanted her to come along? Edrie wondered. Arn, she was of about as much use to him as—

"Got you!" Lammond cried, springing from her side.

A few quick steps took him into an alleyway from which he emerged with a cursing street urchin, his long fingers fastened hard to the boy's ear. But as soon as they stepped from the darker shadows of the alley into the street and the urchin could recognize his captor, his mouth shut and he stood placidly in Lammond's grip.

"I wonder," Lammond said. "What's Johnny Tow up to this eve?"

The urchin quickly shook his head. "Didn't have nothin' to do with Tow, yer lordship, sir. I swear."

"Didn't say you did," Lammond told him.

The boy hung his head.

"What's your name?"

"Tappy, yer lordship, sir."

"I'm no lord," Lammond said.

Edrie blinked at the dark tone to her companion's voice. Didn't like the lordfolk, did he?

"Beggin' yer pardon, yer . . . uh, sir," Tappy mumbled.

Lammond nodded. "No harm done—Tappy, was it?"

The urchin nodded eagerly, an odd mixture of reverence and fear in his features as he looked at Lammond.

"We're looking for a fishergirl," Lammond went on, "and we think she came into Lowtown with Johnny."

Tappy nodded again. "That she did, sir. Johnny tried to net her—planned to rob her an' then sell her to a hussyhall."

"Did he now."

The darkness had returned to Lammond's voice, Edrie noted, but with it directed to Johnny Tow instead of himself, Tappy didn't appear to be nearly so frightened.

"Yes, he did, sir. But she served him! Turned into a ball of fire an' near' burned him to a crisp, she did. She's a bleedin' witch, sir, this fishergirl. Dath, but Johnny's boys did run!"

"And where did she go when they'd left her?" Lammond asked.

Tappy shrugged. "Don't know, sir, an' that's Dath's own truth. Nobody wants to watch the likes of *her* going by."

He seemed to consider what he'd just said and to whom he was saying it. Edrie could see the cogs whirl in his head. Best not to badmouth someone that Lammond was interested in—just in case she turned out to be his friend.

"Beggin' yer pardon, sir," he added, "but that's just what I've heard said."

Lammond nodded. "Thank you for your candor, Tappy."

"My what, sir?"

Lammond shook his head. Rather than answering, he took a coin from his pocket and pressed it into the boy's hand.

"Off with you," he said.

Not until the urchin was swallowed by the shadows of another alleyway, his quick footsteps fading, did Lammond turn to Edrie.

"A witch," he said. "What do you think of that, Edrie Doonan?"

"What's to think? There's no surprise there—not for either of us, I'm thinking."

"That our Ann Netter is a witch, or that the Lowtowners presume her to be one?"

Edrie said nothing. What was the point in arguing the fine points when they both knew what they knew? Lammond merely liked the sound of his own voice, the play of his tongue on the words. He might not care for the lordfolk, but he had some of their airs all the same.

Lammond nodded. "It doesn't matter. Witch, or merely supposed witch, she'll still be in danger."

"The Lowtowners appear to be too afraid of her to hurt her," Edrie said. "At least for tonight."

"You're correct, of course. It takes time for them to gather their courage. But I don't think our quarry remains in Lowtown anyway."

Edrie remembered what Owen had told her.

"The Hill," she said.

"I'm afraid you're right. She has an interest in Aron Corser, it seems."

Aron Corser. Whose witch-finders had already taken young Jackin this afternoon.

"We must—"

Lammond shook his head, interrupting her. "Not we," he said. "I think it best if I go on alone from this point."

"But—"

"Can you make it back to your inn by yourself?"

"Yes, but—"

"The Lowtowners have seen you with me—they'll leave you alone."

"I'm not worried about Lowtowners."

Lammond nodded. "I know. You're worried about a fishergirl and Jackin Toss."

"He's a good lad. Not like the others."

"No?"

"Well, not much," Edrie amended.

"If I find him, I'll bring him back as well. What I need from you is a pair of horses, saddled and provisioned, waiting for me on Bellsilver Lane at the foot of the Hill, in case the night's work takes a messier turn than I'd like and I find I need to take a week or two of the country air. We'd be in a hurry, you see."

"Yes. Of course I can do that. But—"

"But, but. You'd be a poor bargain for the guard, always asking questions."

Edrie wouldn't let him tease her question away.

"Why are you doing this?" she asked.

"You mean, what's in it for Lammond d'es Teillion?"

Edrie nodded. It was impossible to read his features in the poor lighting, but she saw him shrug.

"No matter what I say," he told her finally, "you'd try to second-guess it. Leave it at this. There are those in need and I have chosen to help them. Let that be enough."

Another question rose in Edrie, but she cut it off before speaking it aloud. She thought about what she knew of him and still came up with next to nothing. He was a romantic swashbuckler in the eyes of the town, one with the hint of a dark shadow in his past which only added to his mystique, and that was the sum total of her knowledge of him as well. But he had helped Ann before. And his manner with the urchin just now, that had not been the manner of an evil man.

She would have to trust him.

"I'll have the horses," she said. "Ready and waiting."

"Then wish me luck," he said.

Before she could speak, he turned, stepped into the alleyway and appeared to simply vanish. Edrie could see nothing of him, could hear no footfall. Her fingers began to shape the Sign of Horns. When she caught herself doing that, she angrily stuck her hands in the pockets of her skirt.

"Luck," she called softly after him.

Then she turned and began the trudging walk back to the inn to ready the horses.

28

THE BELLING OF the stag called Tom into the dream again, and it wasn't good.

It never was.

While his body, numbed by alcohol, lay twitching and shivering in a Lowtown alley, he stood alone on a desolate stretch of moor. The hills ran off into lost distances on every side of him, wave upon wave of shadowed grey, swaying under the watchful eye of a swollen moon. The wind bit at his tattered clothes, carrying a sharp tang of sea air from a shoreline too distant to see. Voices called to him in the night, a chorus of ghosts carrying a wordless song on the wind's stinging breath.

And he stood alone, except for the standing stone before him.

The grey rock crackled with a witchy blue fire, throwing shadows across his features as he looked at the face etched in its stone. Its mouth was open; its song was an echo of the ghostsong carried on the wind. Its eyes regarded him without recrimination, but guilt still snapped at his soul like a chase of feral hounds.

The pack would come soon, as it always did. The dogs of his penitence, grown rabid by his presence in this place.

The green.

And she would watch from her stone, for watching was all she could do, year upon year as the seasons spun. The seasons turned, but it was men and women who were the wheels of the world, cogs in a clockwork machine that timed its motion to the ebb and flow of their lives. The wheels turned, following the seasons, but she was dislodged from her rightful place in the mechanism that was the world, forever trapped in her stone.

Here. In the green.

The ghostsong faded until it was only one voice. Her voice. Singing to him. Striving to wash away his guilt. But he was deaf to all but the voice of the pack that hounded him.

He could hear them coming now, their lean feral bodies streaking through the bell heather, their howls entwined until it was a single sound, rushing towards him across the hills.

He would flee, as he always did. Because he wasn't man enough to face them. Because he'd spent his courage in war and whiskey. Though he longed for an end to it, he was too much the coward to face what he had done. To right past wrongs.

He meant to. Each time the dream came, called up by the belling voice of that red-flanked stag, he meant to. But then he would hear the pack, and he would flee again.

She would watch from the stone as he went pell-mell through the heather, stumbling along as fast as he could drag his lamed leg behind him. She would watch from the stone, her gaze piercing the night with depth, while he fled through the flat landscape that his one good eye showed him.

Don't run, her ghostvoice would call after him.

You did no wrong, that voice meant. But he heard only: be a coward no longer.

And he would flee—floundering through the heather, panting like a dog himself as he scrabbled his way up one steep incline, staggered down another. Fleeing. Fleeing. Until the hounds were all around him, their baying and growls louder than the rumble of summer storm thunder.

And he would flee.

Until a root caught him and he tripped.

Or until he fell from sheer exhaustion.

And then the hounds would close in, jaws slavering, his cowardice plain in each glinting eye. They would trap him in a circle that only hope could penetrate, but he had no hope either. That, too, had been swallowed by war and whiskey. And by the deed that had driven him into their arms.

But before the hounds could close in on him, before their teeth tore at his unworthy flesh, their ranks would part and the stag would be there, red-flanked and dark-eyed, its tines ringed with witch-fire. The moon always in its eyes. And wisdom. And mystery.

I, too, lost all hope once, it would tell him. *I, too, suffered.*

Those dark eyes, so deep with sympathy and understanding that the weight of their gaze was a pain in itself. For her eyes were there as well; her eyes were a part of that gaze, her sympathy and understanding.

And that he couldn't bear.

He would tear at his rags, exposing his throat and chest to the hounds. But they backed away from the presence of the stag and its mystery. They fled the moon in its eyes. Bowed before its wisdom.

That was how the dream went, ever and again. Except tonight. Tonight, while his body lay in its whiskey stupor, nested in the refuse of Lowtown, he heard the ghostsong, and he heard the hounds, but before he could flee, the witch-fire rose higher about the longstone, crackling and hissing. It leapt the distance between grey rock and where he stood.

Her face was still there, trapped in its stone prison, her calm gaze watching him, but there was another woman watching him as well, looking out at him from her eyes.

The witch.

Her voice joined the fading ghostsong.

He shook his head, willing her from him. The dream was terrible enough, each time the same, but he couldn't bear for her to change it. Because he deserved no less than its punishment. Though he fled it, though he drank an ocean of whiskey to keep it at bay, it was still fitting and just for the night to bring it to him.

"Go away," he said.

And then he called on the power of names.

"Angharad. Leave me alone."

But already the dream had changed. The menace was gone and he was left with only the serene features etched in the longstone. The moon hanging high above.

And wisdom.

And mystery.

He bowed his head and wept, and was still weeping when he woke in Lowtown. Woke to the stink of his body and the mire of the alley. Woke to the pain in his heart that tore great racking sobs from his chest.

He lifted his head to the night sky, framed by the crooked buildings of Lowtown on all sides.

"Damn her," he cried. "Oh, Arn." The old name came easily to his lips, the stern judgmental strictures of Dath forgotten. "Damn her . . ."

He clawed his way to his feet and leaned against a filthy wall, shivering as though fevered. A headache drummed between his temples. His empty eye socket burned. His lame leg held a muscle cramp that left it stiff and aching.

Understanding, was she? Full of sympathy?

Well, he would show her.

He staggered out of the alleyway, drawn to her like a bee to honey, by the secret they shared. By the green. He looked down at his hands, the grimed flesh hiding a witch's fingerbones, the marrow of the Summerlord's gift.

Curse, he amended. Hafarl's curse.

For he had sight, but no magic. No wisdom.

Still the green drew him to her. The cogs of their lives clicked against each other in the machine that was the world. And all he could do was follow.

29

THE DARK PEAKS and gables of Aron Corser's house loomed up at Angharad out of the night. Watching from the back lane near Corser's stables, she studied the building and its surrounding land. She could spy no sign of guards or witch-finders. There were no lights in the windows, the structure standing private in the darkness, its secrets hidden—from the eyes of housey-folk, at any rate, though not from the Summerborn, for Angharad could sense Jackin's presence, somewhere behind those stone and wood walls.

He was still alive.

Thank you, Arn, she called silently skyward, for this small blessing.

The moon returned her gaze with silence, but not, Angharad sensed, with indifference. She returned her attention to Corser's house, seeking further.

Jackin's presence was a small flickering blue spark that she could see with her mind's eye. But, as her witchy sight took her further into the building, she sensed something more than just the sleeping witcheries of the kidnapped boy inside. There was another witchery in that house. A deeper enchantment. A darker one.

She shivered when she realized what it must be.

The green death.

It had to be the *glascrow*.

Angharad wrapped her arms around herself to keep from trembling. She had the courage to attempt to rescue the boy. But the *glascrow*. . . . This close to the object of her search, doubts arose once more.

She heard Tarasen's voice in her mind.

Find it.

That she had now done.

Wake it.

Oh, Ballan—how could she dare?

Banish it.

Surely she wasn't strong enough? Surely, if she had such power, it would have manifested itself in a hundred ways before this time? But it hadn't. She carried a threefold gift in her bloodlines, and so she was thrice-blessed by the gods: as a tinker, Ballan, the Lord of Broom and Heather, watched over her; her witchy Summerblood was a gift of Harfarl; as a harper, the Moonmother Arn was her muse. But all she had was small magics—ghosts of what her kind once wielded, a mere echo of their ancient enchantments.

How could she hope to prevail against the horror of that silver and ebony puzzle-box when just the memory of the pattern on its lid was enough to leave her shaking and weak?

She felt the darkness stir inside her, straining at the bonds she had imposed upon it.

Broom and Bloody Heather—*how?*

Because there was no one else, she realized. The thought made her feel a little sick, but it strengthened her as well. She could only do her best—do her best, and hope, and not think about failure except to use the reminder of it to push her on.

So she capped her fear with a memory of what would
be lost if she didn't try.

The green.

The Middle Kingdom of the kowrie that stretched its
fingers into the soul of each Summerborn.

She shut her mind to the insidious whispering of the
shadows that the *glascrow* had set inside her. Squaring her
shoulders, she left the sheltering shadow of the stable
wall and set off across the lawn towards the house. Part
way there, a shape dislodged itself from the darkness of a
hedge.

Angharad knew a sharp blade of fear—it sliced down
her nerves like cold fire—then she went down on one
knee and wrapped her arms around the furry neck of
Aron Corser's pet hoyer.

Magger whined softly against her cheek.

"I told you I'd come back," she whispered to him.

A last hug and she stood to face the house once more.

She crept closer, the hoyer ranging at her side. When
she reached a first floor window, she moved her hand
along its width, an inch or so away from the window
frame, searching for presence of witch-wards.

Nothing.

"Where are they?" she asked Magger.

The hoyer whined softly.

Sleeping?

She closed her eyes and let her witchy sight travel inside the house once more, widening its focus so that it
looked for more than witcheries. She sensed a cat sleeping by the kitchen hearth directly across from the window
where she stood, its dreams twitchy as it chased fancied
mice in its sleep. From a little further away, in a room just
off the kitchen, she sensed human sleepers. The cook
and her helpers, Angharad supposed.

Through the house her witchy sight ranged, marking
the dreams of sleeping servants on the ground and third

floors. On the second floor she found those of the lady of the house and a child. Then a man's—his sleep was shallow, the taste of his dreams bitter. That would be the master of the house, for she could sense the dark shadow of the *glascrow*'s presence in the same room.

But there was no sign of the witch-finders. She turned to the shaggy beast at her side and put a whispered question to him. Magger whined another reply.

He didn't know what had happened to them. One moment they were in the house, the next gone. Gone out, he supposed. Away through the front door, while he was waiting for her here in the back.

To chase down more witches for their master, she thought. Perhaps they were chasing her down—following the trail of rumor and speculation that she'd left behind her in Lowtown.

Gathering her courage anew, Angharad tried the window, but it wouldn't budge. She moved along the back of the house until she came to the door that led into the kitchen. Trying it, she found it unlocked.

"Will you come?" she whispered to the hoyer.

Magger sat down on his haunches, looking glum.

Angharad touched the hoyer's furry brow. "Wait for me then. As soon as I've found the boy, I'll send the pair of you away."

She'd give the boy directions to Farmer Perrin and hope that the goodwill he'd shown her extended to her friends as well. Giving Magger's fur a last ruffle, she eased the door open wider and ghosted her way inside.

With her witchy sight she had no trouble making her way through the unfamiliar layout of the kitchen. A false try opened a door into a pantry. Another to stairs that led upwards. The third door opened onto a stairwell that led down. That was where she sensed Jackin's thoughts—under the house where the urchin was secreted in its basement.

She stepped softly down the stairs, searching for both the thoughts of human guards or the tell tale enchantment of a witch-ward, but found neither. At the bottom of the stairs she found herself in a large room that seemed to be mostly a storage area for various household goods, kegs of ale and an immense collection of wine racks, filled with hundreds of bottles. On the far side of the room she spied a barred door.

Crossing the room, she paused by the door, seeking out the sleeping minds above her. There was no change in their dream patterns. She cast her witchy sight out further, around the house and its grounds, and found only Magger's anxious thoughts—the hoyer sitting where she'd left him—and further out, in the stables, the thoughts of two sleeping men that she assumed were grooms. There was none of the cold sparking thoughts that she sensed from the witch-finders in the sleeping pair.

She took a quick steadying breath, then unbarred the door, freezing at the scrape of the wood bar as she hoisted it free of its slots. The door itself creaked alarmingly when she opened it, but a quick survey with her witchy sight assured her that no one had heard. Beyond the door lay a short passageway with a number of doors leading off from it set into either wall.

Broom and Heather. The man had his own private dungeon.

Jackin's presence called out to her from a cell near the end.

This was too easy, Angharad thought as she made her way down the short passage.

Her nervousness grew as she approached the cell. The door here was simply barred with a length of iron set in paired slots on either side of the doorjamb. The metal made her uncomfortable, but she was no kowrie. She could touch iron, for all the discomfort it caused as it resonated with her Summerblood. But while she handled it, she lost her witchy sight.

She scraped it free in darkness, momentarily blinded, nerves shrieking, until she laid it aside. Her witchy sight returned, flooding her mind with the images of her surroundings. She listened for any disturbance above, but heard nothing. A small white face stared at her through the grated window of the door.

"Who . . . ?" Jackin began.

He fell silent as Angharad raised a finger to her lips.

Bracing herself for the darkness to come, she laid her hands on the iron door and pulled it open. She breathed a sigh of relief when she'd pulled it far enough so that Jackin could slip out and she could let go once more. Again, vision returned to her. Again, she searched for sounds of discovery above.

Still nothing.

She looked into the cell and saw that its walls were stone—that was why she'd been able to sense the boy. If the whole chamber had been paneled with iron sheeting, Jackin could have remained in it forever and a day and she'd still not have sensed his presence.

She touched Jackin's arm as he slipped out of the cell and brought her mouth close to his ear.

"If ever you learned a hunter's silent step," she whispered, "remember it now."

Jackin nodded. "Who are you?" he asked, pitching his voice as softly as her own.

"A friend. I've come to help you."

"Won't do no good," he replied. "Soon as I'm back in Lowtown, his witch-finders'll nab me again. He"—Jackin's eyes filled with revulsion and fear— "he wants my *fingers.*"

"I know. I've another friend that might help you."

She told him about Magger, waiting by the back door,

and gave him the description of how to reach Billy Perrin's farm.

"I know him," Jackin replied. "Seen him in the market. I didn't know he was a witch-lover."

There was a certain tone to the boy's voice that made Angharad give him a sharp look.

"And what better person for a witch to go to for help?"

"I'm no witch," Jackin protested.

"No? Then what are you doing here?"

"I . . ." He looked down at his fingers.

"Can you see in the dark?" Angharad asked. "Can you hear singing in the night—the belling of stags and the song of the green?"

"It . . . it's not real . . ."

Angharad touched a hand to his cheek. "It's a gift," she said. "Not a curse.

"So you say."

"So I say," Angharad told him firmly.

Jackin shrugged.

"I've a question for you," she said. "I'm looking for a puzzle-box." She described the *glascrow* to him. "Have you seen anything like that in here?"

It was the best way she could think of to ask if Corser had tried the box on him yet without alarming the boy.

"I've seen nothing but the witch-finders—and now you. What's it worth?"

"A great deal."

"Well, if it's worth good gold, and someone's stolen it, then the Upright Man'll have it."

The Upright Man? she thought. Did Corser run those gangs of urchin thieves in Lowtown as well? Perhaps Johnny Tow had been working for him then, rather than on his own as he'd claimed.

"I could ask around for you," Jackin said, "though it means going back into Lowtown."

Angharad shook her head. "No. Go now—to Perrin's. I'll follow you upstairs, but then I have other business."

"You won't come with me?"

"I can't."

"I could help," Jackin said. "You helped me—it'd only be fair."

Shadows stirred deep inside her. Exposing the boy to the perils of the *glascrow* would be anything but fair, Angharad thought.

"No," she told him.

"But . . ."

Angharad merely gave him a push down the passage. It wasn't until they reached the main chamber of the basement that she heard the scrape of metal against metal behind her. A door opening.

Ballan see her for a fool! How could she have been so stupid? In the dungeon of a witch hunter there *would* be cells, sheeted with iron to block the sight and powers of a witch. She'd been so eager to find Jackin that she hadn't thought to look in the other cells from which she could read no signs of life. What better place for the witch-finders to wait for her than hidden in an iron cell where her witchy sight couldn't spy them out?

"Go!" she cried in a loud voice.

Jackin hesitated, until she gave him another shove.

"I'll find you later," she told him. "Just take Magger with you and go!"

Then she turned to face the Staiyon brothers, already feeling the icy presence of their thoughts in her mind. As Jackin fled across the room and up the stairs, she called up her witchfire and the rowan staff in her hand flared with a blinding light.

"A pretty display," Dagor told her.

"Most impressive," Hoth agreed.

"Pity it won't do you any good," Dagor said.

The witch-finders stood there grinning at her, dressed like twins again in black hunting leathers—from their tooled knee-high boots to the gloves that each wore, knuckles knobbed with iron studs.

She swung the staff, but Hoth blocked the blow with his forearm. Sparks showered around them. Before she could withdraw the staff, Dagor had grabbed it and wrenched it from her hands. He threw it across the room where it landed in another shower of sparks. His gloves smoked, but the leather was only singed. The witchfire hadn't even come close to reaching his skin.

Angharad reached for the bundle of rowan twigs in her pocket, meaning to ignite them and throw them at their eyes, but Dagor struck her with a blow to her stomach that doubled her over. She dropped to her knees, gasping for air. Hoth caught a fistful of her hair and dragged her face up so that she was forced to look at him.

"Be nice now," he said, "and we'll see that all you lose is your fingers."

Dagor nodded. "Pretty woman like you, you could still make a living in the hussyhalls. There's men that would pay well for the privilege of bedding a witch—even one without her powers."

Angharad spat at him, but the pair only laughed. Dagor wiped the spittle from his cheek. He nodded toward the cells. Hoth yanked her towards them, laughing louder as her nails slid on his leather gear, unable to find purchase or do him any harm.

"You'll have to do better than that, my little scalygirl," he told her.

As he dragged her into a cell, Angharad felt the presence of the cold iron close in around her. Every inch of floor, ceiling and walls was sheeted with the metal. Its suffocating presence brought an icy feeling over her like frost forming on her heart. She found it hard to simply breathe. The green reaches fled and she could feel only the shadow pattern of the *glascrow* moving inside her. Darkness fell across her eyes as her witchy sight was cut off. Hoth pushed her towards the far wall of the cell, where she collapsed on the floor.

Her stomach ached from where he'd hit her. Nausea churned inside her, bringing a raw taste up her throat. Unable to see in the darkness, unable to use her witchy sight, Angharad felt deaf and dumb. Helpless.

"What about the boy?" Dagor said as he lit a torch.

The flare of light momentarily blinded Angharad.

"Let him go," Hoth replied. "Master Corser's not going to care about him—not when he sees the fine fingers we have for him here."

"I'll go fetch him," Dagor said.

As her sight cleared, Angharad watched him go. Then she turned her gaze to Hoth who remained standing in the doorway.

"Well," the witch-finder said. "Whatever will we do to pass the time?"

30

LAMMOND HAD REACHED that part of the lane directly behind Corser's house when he saw Jackin Toss come charging out of the building's rear door as though all the fiends of a Dather's hell were on his heels. Corser's hoyer rose up from the darkness beside the door as the boy burst forth. Lammond waited a long heartbeat for the beast to bring Jackin down, but the dog merely paced the boy as he ran across the lawn. As Jackin neared him, Lammond stepped out from the shadows of the stable and called out to him.

"Been visiting the gentry, then, Jackin?"

Dog and boy came to an abrupt halt. A low growl rumbled in the hoyer's chest, but then he seemed to recognize that Lammond meant no harm. Jackin, however, appeared ready to bolt again.

"You've no reason to fear me, boy," Lammond said.

Jackin breathed Lammond's name, his nervousness all too apparent.

"The same," Lammond replied. "At your service, as it were."

"I didn't do nothing—" Jackin began.

"Never said you did, boy. And I won't keep you long.

All I've got is a simple question for you. Did you see a fishergirl by the name of Ann Netter while you were in yon lord's house?''

Jackin nodded. "She's the one what freed me. But she's not a fishergirl, don't matter how she dresses. She's a witch.''

"And where is she now?''

"She a friend of yours, sir?''

The darkness hid Lammond's frown. "I've a name, boy, not a title.''

"I . . .'' The urchin straightened his shoulders. "I've a name, too.''

Lammond smiled at the boy's boldness. "Well, spoken—Jackin. Now would you mind answering my question?''

"You won't like it, sir—I mean, Lammond. The witch-finders caught her.''

"She rescued you, and then you turned tail on her and ran?''

"She told me to run—me and the dog.''

Lammond glanced down at the hoyer. "This isn't Corser's dog?''

"I think it is,'' Jackin said, "but it seems to like your friend better.''

Lammond gave the dog a considering look and raised his estimation of the witch a notch or two. Bewitched the merchant's dog, had she?

"If you want to help her,'' Jackin said, "you'd better move quick.''

He jerked a thumb over his shoulder to where lights were appearing in Corser's house.

"Why didn't she run with you?'' Lammond asked.

"Said she was looking for something—a stolen puzzle-box.''

"Did she, now.''

Jackin nodded, though Lammond hadn't framed his remark as a question.

"I told her if it was stolen, and if it had any value, it'd be in the Upright Man's hands."

"Did you."

Jackin nodded again.

"Yet she appears to believe Corser has it?"

"Don't know."

"You've been a help," Lammond told him. "Were you to meet her later?"

"She gave me directions to Farmer Perrin's holding—he's the one that has that stand down on—"

"I know the man," Lammond said. "You'd better get going then—you and the dog."

Jackin hesitated. "What are you going to do?" he asked finally.

Lammond smiled. "Go in and take her from the merchant and his pet bully boys—what did you think?"

"Didn't think nothing," Jackin said.

Lammond didn't doubt that Jackin—like the rest of Cathal, except for Veda—wondered about him. They all wanted to know his business, but there wasn't the one had the nerve, or even the plain common sense, to simply come out and ask him. Instead, they watched him with wide eyes wherever he went, quieting as he passed, whispering when he'd gone on by.

"Off you go then, Jackin," he said.

The urchin still hesitated. "Do you want some help?"

"Got your courage back, have you?"

"It's not that. I just . . ."

Lammond stepped forward and put a hand on the boy's shoulder. "I know," he said. "You panicked—happens to us all, Jackin, so there's no need for shame. You go on to Perrin's farm and we'll be along, by and by."

"But . . ."

Lammond gave Jackin's shoulder a squeeze. "You

don't think one fat merchant and a pair of preening witch-finders are going to cause me that much trouble now do you?''

"I . . . no. I suppose not. At least, if you don't think they will . . .''

"If you see your friend Edrie down on Bellsilver, waiting for me with a pair of horses, you can tell her that I've things well in hand.''

"I will, sir—ah, Lammond.''

"There's a lad. Now, not a word of tonight's work is to leave your lips—do I have your promise?''

He read Jackin's face as surely as though he could read the boy's mind: how could he talk of tonight without getting himself into so much trouble with the guard that he'd not see the light of day for a very long time again—except from the windows of their gaol? There were laws in Cathal—even if they only protected those who could afford to pay the wages of those who enforced them.

"I promise,'' Jackin said.

Lammond nodded. "Until later, then,'' he said.

Without waiting for a response, he turned to consider the house once more. He could hear Jackin shuffling his feet in place behind him, still hesitating.

"You'll be the most help by passing on my message to Edrie,'' Lammond said without turning.

The boy ran off down the lane then, Corser's hoyen pacing him.

Bewitched the dog, did she? Lammond thought. It made him wonder how she was at bewitching men. Though, naturally—even if their brains were no larger than the shelled peas Lammond assumed them to be—they would have taken precautions. Bound her with iron or locked her in an iron-plated room. Laid upon her bosom the four-tined symbol of the Dead God Dath. And didn't witch-finders have wards to protect them against the Summerborn? Something about their own abilities being a gift from Lithun?

No matter. Neither iron nor holy symbol nor witch-ward meant a fig to him.

Smiling to himself, he started off across the lawn.

31

TOM HID IN the mouth of an alleyway off Bellsilver Lane at the foot of the Hill and listened to the tale the street urchin spilled to the innkeeper. He'd first hidden there when he had spied Edrie Doonan standing on the street, holding the reins of a provisioned horse in either hand. He watched her for a few moments, marking the nervous looks she cast about herself.

What are you up to, Edrie? he wondered. Out poking about in Lowtown with Lammond d'es Teillion earlier, and now here, as nervous as a merchant who's heard that Tave Maspic has marked his goods for plunder?

Tom wished he weren't so drunk. Perhaps then he could make sense of it all. Or conversely, he wished he were more drunk, so that he wouldn't care. But tonight, there didn't seem to be a choice but to walk in between the two.

Half-deciding to step forward and speak with her, he'd remained hidden when he heard the patter of quick footsteps as Jackin Toss arrived. The urchin was out of breath from his run down a back lane of the Hill. What had stopped Tom, however, was neither the urchin's arrival, nor Edrie, but the presence of the hoyer that ran at Jackin's side.

Never mind the beast's vicious nature—Tom had seen them on the battlefields of the Continent. In the Green Isles, hoyers were worth a small fortune, and this one, without a doubt, belonged to Aron Corser. No one else in Cathal had one, which was the principal reason Corser had acquired the savage creature in the first place. Acquired it and tamed it to his hand and no other.

So what was it doing in the company of a street urchin that Corser's own witch-finders had dragged off this very afternoon?

Tom's head ached, trying to think of it all—then ached some more as he listened to Jackin's tale. None of it made sense.

Edrie and d'es Teillion working together to rescue a witch?

Tom could still remember lying on his back in an alleyway, the hard stone under him, the feel of the the swordsman's blade toying with the rags of his jacket . . .

Tell me a story . . .

D'es Teillion had a hunger for witch-lore. For what reason, Tom didn't know—didn't care—but with what he knew of the man, the lore d'es Teillion acquired would never be put to good use. Not when Tom considered the things d'es Teillion had done.

The swordsman saw him as a drunk—which Tom was; as a beggar man with a faint touch of the green curse upon him—and Tom admitted to that as well. But what d'es Teillion didn't see was that once this same drunken beggar had been a soldier, serving overseas. He had seen d'es Teillion go about his bloody work then . . .

This was the man who had a sudden compassion for a witch and went to rescue her? The man they called the Gentry Butcher on the Continent because he only took on assassinations of the wealthy and those in positions of power? They said he had no heart, and with what Tom had seen, he didn't doubt the truth of that rumor for a moment.

If he closed his eyes, he could see it again: a late night on a foreign street, and there was old Tom sitting drunk in an alleyway—not a beggar then, nor even so old, just another soldier on leave who'd had a pint too many to make his way back to camp. D'es Teillion stopped the lord and his two guards on the street, directly across from the mouth of the alleyway in which Tom was sitting.

The guards died first—d'es Teillion killed them quickly, almost negligently.

And then he toyed with the lord.

Cut the poor bugger to pieces.

No clean death, that. It had been torture, plain and simple. Tom knew nothing of the man who died that night, but what evils must a man commit to deserve such a death?

And his murderer was the man who went to rescue Angharad tonight?

Meant to have her blood bathe his blade, more likely. Meant to steal all her witch-lore, then leave her lying in some back lane, bleeding from a hundred wounds. And who would care? She was just a witch, wasn't she?

But whether he wanted to or not, Tom cared.

She'd been kind to him. For no reason except that it was in her nature to do so. How was she to know the pain she woke in him? How was she to understand how the green could be a gift to some, but a curse to others?

He could feel it stir inside him. The belling of the stag, ringing in his inner ear. If he closed his eyes, Arn's light shone bright against his eyelids, as it did from the eyes of the stag.

Moonlight.

And wisdom.

And mystery.

Oh, Tom's head ached.

How could he help her? He wasn't a soldier any more—he wasn't even a man. How could he stand up against d'es Teillion's sword? It was a fool's dream to even consider it.

But he remembered her kind eyes.

He remembered the longstone in the green and the face that was etched in its stone. Other eyes—just as kind as the witch's, but infinitely more dear to him.

The one those eyes belonged to . . .

He had failed her. And no matter what he did, he could never pay the debt he owed her. The past was irrevocable. Done was done, as his dad used to say, before—

Enough, Tom told himself. Done *was* done.

He watched Jackin hurry off, the hoyer still accompanying him. Edrie stood with her horses, gazing up the lane to where Corser's house stood on the Hill.

Done was done.

But while the past couldn't be changed, could not past wrongs be set right? If he'd failed the one, could he not try to help the other? Might that not balance some scale? Might not the dreams finally haunt him no more?

Oh, he would fail—he knew that. But if he could at least help Angharad escape . . . if he could buy her enough time to win free—even if the coin paid was his own life . . . would the attempt itself not count?

I, too, lost all hope, the stag never tired of telling him. *I, too, suffered.*

As had Angharad, he realized. But must she suffer more?

He wondered if he would have the time to tell her that he had lied to her. That he remembered that traveler's tale not for the strength of the love that Cony and the beekeeper's daughter had shared, as he had told her he had, but for the same reason she remembered it as well: for what he had lost. For the sadness.

All he had was the memory of love—ringed black and shadowed by what he had done.

He moved deeper down the alleyway, taking a circuitous route that would bring him up the Hill, but well out of Edrie Doonan's sight.

All he had was neither the love nor the sadness, but the knowledge of his own cowardice which he hadn't been able to spend in either war or the bottle.

Perhaps he could spend it now.

32

ARON CORSER WASN'T long in coming to see the new Summerborn that his witch-finders had acquired for him.

"She's a pretty one, isn't she?" he said as Dagor made way for him in the doorway.

Angharad studied him in the torchlight. So here was the monster. A fat, pompous merchant, with pig's jowls and a weasel's shifty eyes. In his pudgy hands lay the fate of the green.

She could have wept at the injustice of it, but was determined to give them no additional pleasure at the indignity she suffered. A tinker was used to the jeers of the housey-folk. They had imprisoned her body, she was damned if she'd give them her heart or her soul.

Oh, but to lose the green . . .

To lose the music her fingers called from her harp's strings . . .

"A pretty one, yes," Dagor said, "but dangerous beyond the confines of this chamber."

The witch-finder hadn't touched her while they waited for Hoth to bring the merchant down from his bed. He'd merely stood in the doorway and kept up a cheerful one-sided conversation as to what she could expect from this night's work, smirking at the stoic face she put forward.

"Dangerous," Corser said with a titter. "Oh, yes, I know that. Though she's not so dangerous now—is she?" He nodded to Hoth. "Still, best get to it and remove her witcheries immediately. We wouldn't want her to win her way free, somehow, before we'd first procured those lovely bones."

Angharad couldn't suppress the shiver that traveled up her spine.

Her witcheries.

Her fingerbones.

Oh, Ballan, give me strength to endure.

Hoth drew a long knife from its sheath at his belt. Cruel irony, Angharad thought, as she recognized the steel for what it was—a tinker blade.

"Hold her, Dagor," he said to his brother by the door as he moved further into the cell.

But there was something wrong with Dagor. Hoth and the merchant turned to look at the man's suddenly wide eyes. Dagor's mouth opened, lips trembling convulsively, and then they all saw the long length of steel that protruded from the center of his chest, the cool metal wet with his blood.

Hoth took a step forward, tinker blade raised up in his fist. The sword length withdrew from Dagor's body. The witch-finder pitched forward, striking the metal floor directly at Angharad's feet. Filling the doorway now was Lammond d'es Teillion, bloodied sword held negligently in his hand.

Hoth gave an inarticulate howl and charged the swordsman. Lammond flicked his blade once, and the witch-finder's blade left his hand to clang against the floor—accompanied by the fingers of the hand that had been holding it. A second flicker of the sword and

Hoth's throat was opened. Blood sprayed in wide arcs as the witch-finder lifted his hands to stay the flow. A third flicker of the sword drove the blade straight into Hoth's heart. A moment later he fell to his knees, still clutching his throat, then sprawled over his brother's body.

Lammond turned to Corser. The merchant stood cowering in a corner of the cell. Weaponless, he tugged at the pouch that was tied to his belt. When he had it free, he offered it up to the swordsman.

"T-take it . . ."

Lammond's eyebrows rose to ask the question his voice did not.

"It . . . th-there's a fortune—"

Lammond's sword flickered out once more, cutting the pouch free so that all the merchant held was its strings. The pouch fell to the floor and spilled its contents across the floor. Angharad stared at the tumble of fingerbones that lay there.

"I think not," Lammond said.

"Th-the guard . . ."

"Will do nothing. Who is summoning them? And there are no witnesses, now, are there? Do you think I'll run to tell them of the night's work? Or will your prisoner?"

"I . . . I . . ."

The man fairly blubbered with panic. His eyes bulged, showing their whites. His fat body shook. Looking at him, Angharad could almost feel pity. But then her gaze moved to the spill of fingerbones that lay on the floor of the cell, and all pity fled.

"Such a cozy place you have here," Lammond said. "I'll wager sound doesn't carry far from it. Wouldn't want to trouble your loving family with the screams of those you're torturing here below, now would you?"

"P-please . . ."

The sword in Lammond's hand moved back and

forth in a short arc. From time to time a drop of blood made its way to the very tip and fell free.

"Let me tell you a story," Lammond said. "It might amuse you. There was a man once and he had three sisters. Their father had run off; their mother had died of a sickness—" He gave Corser a serious look. "This will happen, you understand, in the squalor of a slum. A place like Cathal's Lowtown. Though of course, being wealthy, you'd be able to afford the best healers, wouldn't you? So this is all foreign to you."

"I . . . I don't . . ."

"Patience, now. It's not a long story, nor a particularly original one. The man was the youngest child—a good six years junior to the youngest of his sisters. And they were beautiful, those sisters—almost as beautiful as your prisoner, here. Do you know what happened to them?"

"N-no. I . . ."

"Why, lords used them. One was twelve, one was fourteen, and one was fifteen. And the lords used them. Came drunk to the slum where the four of them lived; spied them and thought, won't we have some fun with these urchins? For who would care what they did with these children? Would *you* care, merchant?"

Corser bobbed his head eagerly. "Oh, yes. I would—"

The sword flickered up to dance before the merchant's eyes. Lammond's own gaze was dark with sudden anger.

"Don't lie to me. *Never* lie to me."

"I . . . I . . ."

"You wouldn't care," Lammond said then, continuing in a calm voice once more. "As they didn't. And didn't they have a time, that night? There were six of them—six drunken lords. And when the children protested, why, they'd hit them. Wouldn't you, merchant? To stop their damnable wailing?"

"I . . ."

"And if events grew somewhat out of hand and one of the children were to die . . . well, it was no great loss, was it? Street urchins come a dozen for the penny, don't they? And what if that death were somehow . . . amusing? What if violence grew more appealing than carnal pleasure? Wouldn't it be . . . *interesting* to see how long it took another to die? To cut her once. And again. And again, until she bled from a hundred wounds and still lived? Wouldn't that be something?"

"I . . . I never . . ."

Lammond shrugged. "So they died—all three of them."

He fell silent then, his expression still mild, his gaze fixed on the merchant who continued to cower against the wall, blubbering and sobbing. Back and forth wove the blade in his hand, tip pointed at the floor, the occasional drop of blood still falling from it, glistening in the torchlight.

"And the man?" Angharad asked finally. "The man that was that boy? What happened to him?"

For she understood Lammond's story. She knew whose sisters had died so tragically.

The swordsman glanced at her. "Well, he was lucky, wasn't he? He'd been hidden by his sisters in a cupboard of that hovel, hidden when the lords first came hammering at their door. He got to watch the whole affair through a knothole. He survived."

"Lucky?" Angharad said softly. "I don't think so."

Lammond shrugged again. "It all depends on your perspective, Ann Netter."

Angharad shivered at the calmness of his tone. There was an almost beatific look in his eyes—an otherworldliness that had nothing to do with the green.

"I . . . I don't understand," Corser said finally. "What does . . . does this have to do with me? . . ."

"I think it's rather simple," Lammond said. "You're

all the same, aren't you? Lords and merchants alike. You buy whatever you need, and if you can't buy it, then you take it."

"I never hurt a child like that . . ."

Corser's voice trailed off as he glanced at Angharad.

Lammond's eyebrows rose quizzically. "Nor a witch?"

"B-but . . ."

"Of course," Lammond said. "They're not human, are they? Doesn't matter their age. They're witches. *You* would never hurt some poor urchin child, *would* you?"

"I . . ."

"You would never make a profit from the suffering of others, *would* you?"

"I'm . . . sorry . . ."

Lammond smiled. "I'm sure you are—at this moment. But it makes little difference, given your past history, given what you were about to do to this woman in this very room. Though of course it wasn't to be your hands wielding the knife blade, was it? You'd merely stand by and . . . watch."

"No. That is . . ."

"We're much alike, you and I," Lammond said. "We both make our livings from the suffering of others." He lifted his sword until its tip was inches from Corser's eyes. "I hire myself out to rid the world of vermin such as yourself. It's"—he smiled—"what I do. Happily, there are those who will pay me for my work. Pay me well."

"Wh-who . . . ?"

"Hired me to kill you? Why, no one. You brought this on yourself. Occasionally—when I'm bored, and there doesn't come an assignment for a while—I work for myself. For you see, whether I'm paid to or not, I mean to rid all the world of your kind."

Angharad had been studying him as he spoke. He was mad, of course. It was a terrible thing that had happened to his sisters—a terrible thing that the six-year-old he had been had seen what he'd seen. He had survived, yes, but not with an intact mind.

She considered the merchant, trying to decide if she should attempt to stay Lammond's killing stroke. But when she looked at the fingerbones spilled upon the floor of the cell, when she remembered his amusement as his men had been ready to go about their work, she found that she couldn't.

But there was one thing she needed to know.

"Lammond," she said.

As he glanced at her, she caught the faint glint of madness behind his darkening gaze. She remembered what Johnny Tow had told her.

There's a meanness in him that's easy to miss until it turns on you.

No, she wouldn't try to stop him.

"Please," he said. "Don't interrupt me, Ann Netter."

"It's . . . it's not that. It's just—"

She swallowed thickly. Just thinking of the *glascrow* made her break out in a sweat.

"The merchant has something I need," she said.

"Does he, now."

Angharad nodded. "A puzzle-box."

"A black and silver puzzle-box?" Lammond asked.

"Yes. How did you . . . ?"

"I've seen it," Lammond said. "Would you like to have it? I know where it is."

"Yes. That is . . ."

"Oh, it's no trouble at all. One moment while I—"he turned suddenly, impaling Corser on the tip of his blade, then putting his weight behind the thrust so that the sword went straight through the merchant's body—"fin-ish this."

Angharad turned away. Corser wailed, clapping his hands over the hole in his chest as Lammond withdrew the blade Corser dropped to his knees. Blood spewed from between his fingers, washing his hands and chest. A moment later, he toppled over to lie on the floor with his witch-finders, as dead as the pair of them.

"Come along then," Lammond said.

Angharad lifted her gaze to his face. The mad glint was hidden once more. He spoke as though they were simply browsing through a marketplace and he wanted her to see something interesting at another stall. As he stepped towards her, obviously meaning to give her a hand up, she scrambled quickly to her feet.

She couldn't face touching him—did he see that in her eyes?

If he did, he gave no indication.

"The . . . the bones," she said.

He gave her a surprised look. "You *want* them?"

"No. I . . . They should be burned, so that others won't use them."

"Of course."

"Only I can't . . ."

"Bear to touch them?"

Angharad nodded.

"I'll get them for you."

Arn, how was it possible? How he could so calmly kill those three men, then act as though the deed had never been done? How could he be so cold, yet in the next instant, appear warm and understanding?

She stood to one side, hugging herself, as he carefully returned the bones to their pouch.

"Shall I carry them?" he asked, as he straightened up.

"Please."

Outside the cell, her witchy sight returned to her with a rush. It was as though she'd been blind and could suddenly see. No, it was more than recovering from blindness. It was losing all her senses, all the depth and meaning from life, and suddenly having them returned to her—all at once.

Her gaze focused on the pouch that Lammond held. With the return of her witcheries, she realized that it hadn't been the *glascrow* calling to her from the merchant's house, but rather his bag of fingerbones.

Their bright magics, sullied.

Their green, faded and dead.

Become a darkness, each witch's pain worked into the marrow of each bone so that they twinned the aura that hung about the *glascrow*.

For wasn't this mutilation but another kind of green death?

She leaned against the wall, steadying herself for a long moment, before she could follow Lammond across the storage area of the wine cellar. It wasn't until she was upstairs and out on the lawn with him, that she remembered she'd left her staff behind.

"My staff," she said.

With her witchy sight returned, she could see in the darkness, could see his smile.

"Your witch-wood staff?" he asked. "The white rowan wood?"

"You know?"

"That you're not Ann Netter, the simple fishergirl? All along, I'm afraid."

"Then why have you helped me?"

Lammond shrugged. "Why not? I've nothing against witches—only lords. Besides, I've need of a witch."

All the mismatched pieces came together for Angharad then. It wasn't Aron Corser, monster though he was, who had the green death. It was Lammond. Arn help her, how was she to prevail against him?

"You have the *glascrow,"* she said.

"The what?"

"The puzzle-box."

"I know where it is," he said.

"What do you mean to do with it? You said you have

nothing against witches. If that's true, then why do you want to kill the green?"

"The green? Is that the supposed otherworld of the kowrie—Hafarl's realm?"

Angharad nodded.

"I don't want to kill it. I just want to kill lords. All of them. I've heard that this box has a secret in it that can do just that."

"It's not true. You won't hurt the housey-folk with it. You'll just hurt my people. You'll destroy the green. You'll take away the last traces of wonder and magic that are left in this world."

Lammond gave her a long silent glance, then his shoulders lifted and fell.

"Wonder?" he asked. "Magic? I don't see any in this world. I never have, not since . . ."

His voice trailed off, but Angharad knew what he'd been about to say: not since his sisters died. For even urchins in the slums could know wonder and magic, if there was love between them.

Then she thought of what Lammond was saying. He could bring her to the *glascrow*. Well, what more did she need? Hadn't Tarasen told her to find it?

Now she could.

No matter what he expected of her, or of the *glascrow*, once she held it in her hands, she could attempt what she'd come here to do.

Wake it.

Banish it.

She could at least try.

"Never mind," she told him. "Take me to it and we'll see what we see."

Lammond smiled. "You're thinking to play a trick on me."

Angharad regarded him seriously.

"I came here to wake it," she said, "and that's what you want of me too, isn't it?"

"Wake it," Lammond agreed, "with your triad magic, and then send its witcheries out to kill them all."

"I promise to wake it," Angharad said, "but once its power is woken, I can make no more promises. I was told that it can't be controlled."

"Then how did you mean to defeat it?"

"I think it requires a sacrifice," she replied, struggling to keep her voice steady. "I think I will have to give myself to it, to die while it is in me, so that it dies with me."

"I can do that," Lammond said softly.

Angharad merely regarded him. That would do no good. He didn't have the Summerblood in him. If a sacrifice was required, it was required of one Summerborn.

"If it will do as I bid," Lammond added, "then I will gladly die for it."

That wasn't quite what she'd meant, Angharad thought.

"Is there any particular place that would be best to work this magic?" Lammond asked.

"Are there stoneworks near Cathal?"

Lammond nodded. "On the south shore of the bay, above the town. There's a solitary holed stone there that the locals call the Whistling Man for the sound it makes when the wind comes in from the shore and blows through its hole."

"Then that is where we should go," Angharad told him.

33

OLD TOM HEARD everything they said.

When he learned that d'es Teillion would be taking Angharad to the Whistling Man, he moved soundlessly back through the garden, eschewing the rear lane that they would be taking for the broader avenue that ran in front of Corser's house.

This late at night there were no guards about, nor rich folk to call them out, so he made good time as he hobbled down the cobblestone street. The last of his drunkenness was gone now, but by the time he reached the spot where Edrie Doonan was waiting with the two provisioned horses on Bellsilver Lane, he was completely out of breath.

Edrie gave a start at his sudden appearance, then wrinkled her nose when she saw—smelled, was more like it, Tom thought—who it was.

"Lord, but you gave me a fright," Edrie said, obviously trying to put up a good front, though why she'd care what an old drunkard wondered about her business, Tom didn't know.

"Don't"—*huff*—"have much time."

"Tom . . . Naghatty, is it?"

Tom nodded. "The witch," he said. "Angharad." *Huff.* "Do you mean to help her—to *truly* help her?"

Dath! What if he was wrong? What if she was thick as thieves with d'es Teillion?

"Angharad . . . ?" Edrie began, then she nodded. "So that's her real name."

Tom wanted to shake her. Any moment now, and the pair of them would be coming down from Corser's house where he'd left them.

"Do you know of the green death?" he demanded.

"The green death?"

But Tom could see from her eyes that she didn't—no more than he had until he'd overheard Angharad and Lammond discussing it. He told Edrie what he'd heard.

"D'es Teillion has it," Tom finished, "and he means to use Angharad to wake it. He thinks it'll kill all the lords, when what it actually does is kill the green."

"So that's why he's been so helpful," Edrie said. "I should have known better than to trust him."

"He's going to fetch the thing," Tom went on, "then he's taking them both—Angharad and the death—to the Whistling Man. Can you get help?"

"Help? Arn, but you haven't thought this through. Who'd risk themselves against Lammond for a witch? Who'd even help a witch out of the gutter, even if all it took was a hand up?"

Angharad had offered him more than a hand up, Tom thought. She had offered to restore meaning to his life, if he were only willing. And, inadvertently, she'd given him back a sense of worth.

"What of Billy Perrin?" he asked. "Isn't he her friend? I heard her and Jackin talking about him."

"I don't know if Perrin knows she's a witch."

Tom shook his head. "It doesn't matter. Jackin's there. He'll help. Dath, she helped him, didn't she?"

"Will you do it? Will you ride out and bring them to the stone?"

"And what will you be doing?"

"I'll go ahead on my own."

Edrie simply looked at him. "You? Against Lammond?"

"I was a soldier once."

"Once. But look at you now."

He wasn't much to look at, it was true. Dath, he knew it better than anyone. But . . .

Tom took a steadying breath.

"I've the Summerblood, as well," he said.

It was easier to say than he'd thought it would be.

"Do you, now?"

Tom could hear footsteps in the lane.

"They're coming. Will you ride for the farm?"

"I will."

"Then luck go with you."

He started to turn away, but Edrie caught his arm. As he faced her once more, she handed him the reins of one of the horses.

"Let's not give him any more advantage than he already has. Take the horse."

"But . . ."

She read his face, even in the dark, without witchy sight.

"I trust you," she said. "Now go!"

She swung up into the saddle. A moment later, he was mounted as well. Giving her a quick wave, he knocked his heels against the horse's sides and the street was filled with the sudden clatter of horses' hooves on the cobblestones—he riding the one way, Edrie the other.

He passed d'es Teillion and Angharad as they emerged from the lane, head bent over the far side of his mount's neck so that they wouldn't recognize him. He heard d'es Teillion call out after him, but then he was around a street corner and out of sight.

He slowed the horse and straightened up in the saddle.

The Whistling Man, was it?

How long before d'es Teillion arrived, with Angharad and the green death in tow? More to the point, how long before Edrie could bring help? For, brave words though he'd offered the innkeeper, he knew as well as she that there was little he could do against the swordsman.

True, he'd been a soldier, but he was just a drunkard now. Of little good to anyone, little to say for himself.

But he had the Summerblood, didn't he?

In his mind, he heard the belling of that otherworldly stag. And the ghostsong, calling to him. *Her* voice in that song. *Her* eyes looking at him with approval.

For the first time, he understood—truly *heard*—what she said.

You did no wrong.

Not to be a coward any more.

But that he'd done no wrong when he held the blade to her, when the steel cut deep, when the blood flowed . . .

Blood.

What was it about blood . . . the blood of the Summerborn and the ancient stoneworks?

He tried to snag the elusive memory as he rode out of town. His horse's hooves clomped on the shingle beach as they followed the shoreline to where the holed stone of the Whistling Man kept its watch over the tide line. Where it stood and gazed across the dark waters of the Grey Sea.

It was when he saw the stone, when he heard the doleful whistle of the wind through its hole, that he remembered.

34

ANGHARAD SENSED THE *glascrow* as soon as they entered the Gallant Archer, where Lammond had his room. Just entering the common room, she could feel the puzzle-box's emanation. It lay like black smoke on the edges of her thoughts, curling about the vague sparking glows that marked the minds of the inn's patrons.

A malevolent presence, ancient and evil.

Calling to her.

Waiting for her.

Broom and Heather, she thought. How could she not have sensed it before? How could she have missed its taint upon the swordsman when she first met him?

But Lammond wasn't Summerborn. The green death wouldn't affect him as it did her. It wouldn't leave its mark on his soul. And besides, he had his own mark upon him. A death mark. A madness. Well hidden, it was true, but having witnessed it at Corser's house, she knew it would always be plain to her now.

There's a meanness in him . . .

It wasn't until they entered Lammond's room that she saw why she hadn't sensed the *glascrow* itself earlier.

The puzzle-box sat on a table, seeming to gather dark

ness into itself. Beside it was a cast-iron box, its lid standing ajar, in which the *glascrow* must normally be stored. The iron would have kept her from detecting it before.

She tried to ignore its ebony and silver patterning, but it drew her gaze, as surely as it drew the room's shadows to itself. A dark swirling pattern that pulled her down, down, to where her own answering shadows called to her . . .

"So this is your witch."

With an effort, Angharad looked away from the puzzle-box—its pattern still spiraling bleakly through her thoughts—to regard the woman who had spoken. She wore a silky gown, loosely tied about her waist, that did little to hide her voluptuous figure. Noting her exaggerated rouge and use of powder and paints, Angharad marked the woman for a courtesan.

"Veda," Lammond said, nodding towards the woman. "And this is Ann Netter." He was in an obvious good humor. "And there," he added unnecessarily, "is your puzzle-box."

"Does she know what you mean to do with it?" Angharad asked, refusing to turn her gaze back to the table.

The *glascrow* whispered in her mind, calling to the seed it had already planted in her mind through Fenn's scryer.

Come walk the road of shadows, it whispered.

"I do," Veda said, answering for herself.

"We are fellow travelers, Veda and I," Lammond said. "Veda is my . . . agent, I suppose one might call her. Through her work with the upper classes, she learns who I may approach for new assignments."

So she *was* a courtesan, Angharad thought.

"It's all very civilized," Lammond added.

"Why bother?" Angharad asked.

Lammond gave her a puzzled look. "I'm sorry?"

"Why bother taking on assignments, or getting paid to kill gentry? Why not just do it?"

"Well, we need to make a living."

"That doesn't seem like you," Angharad said.

Veda laughed. "How does she know you so well, so quickly?"

Angharad never smiled. "It seems to me you'd be much further along with your goals if you simply went about methodically killing all the gentry in a certain area. When you were done there, you could simply move on to the next."

"It's not that simple," Lammond said.

"I know," Angharad said. "It's not civilized."

"That, too. But how long do you think the gentry would allow me to live if I went about my business in such a crude fashion? They can have no complaint when *they* hire me to do their work for them—and there are *always* lords in need of my talents. Mine and Veda's. Our kind is quite indispensable to them."

Angharad looked away from him, turning her attention to Veda.

"I suppose you have a similar tale of childhood misfortune to tell?" she asked.

She heard Lammond's sharp intake at her side, could feel the dark anger flare in him. Veda's eyes narrowed. She glared at Angharad for a long moment, then her features cleared. She shrugged—a fashionable, easy motion.

"Pity you couldn't have found one with better manners," she said to Lammond, her tone light.

"But find her I did," Lammond replied, his own voice betraying none of his anger. "Triad magic—witch, harper and tinker. What more could one want?"

"No need to go looking for witches," Veda explained to Angharad. "That's what Lammond said. Not when the box will bring them to us."

"Lures them like a moth to flame," Lammond said.

"The man from whom I received the box explained it all to me. I was to take it from its protective casing at regular intervals and merely set it in the air."

"But not for too long," Veda said.

Lammond nodded. "For, given enough exposure to it, it can work its uncomfortable wonders on those without the Summerblood as well."

Now that, Angharad thought, was patently untrue. Tarasen had said . . .

It needs the Summerblood to be kindled.

Tarasen. Who'd told Angharad she must—

Find it.

Now found it was.

Wake it.

Had she ever had a choice to do anything but?

Not since that night by Ballan's Broom—that morning when she spoke with Hafarl's daughter in the woods of Avalarn.

Banish it.

It wasn't until that moment when she spoke with Lammond on the lawn behind Corser's house that she'd truly understood what the attempt would cost her.

She stole a shivering glance at the table where the puzzle-box brooded—calling, calling to her . . .

Come walk in shadow . . .

"I will need my harp," she said.

Lammond nodded. "Of course. We'll fetch it now."

He went to the table and replaced the *glascrow* in its iron casing. Angharad felt an immediate relief, but that faded as soon as she realized that the shadow inside her had grown stronger, whining a darker song across the reaches of her green.

"When we reach the stone," Angharad said, "before we do anything we will burn the fingerbones that Corser collected."

Lammond raised an eyebrow. "I hardly see that you're in a position to demand anything."

"After I've woken the *glascrow* for you, I'll be dead myself. I mean to see the souls of those witches, at least, laid to rest first."

"Lammond, you said there was no danger," Veda said.

"There is none."

But Veda wasn't looking at him. Her gaze had settled on Angharad.

"None to you," Angharad admitted, not sure why she took the time to ease the woman's fears. "Only to my kind. Only to the green. The *glascrow* kills the green, not housey-folk."

"But, Lammond—"

"It will kill lords," he said firmly. "It will kill all the gentry." He gripped the iron box that held the *glascrow* with whitening knuckles. "And then we'll be free, my sweet."

Angharad shook her head. There was no freedom from the demons that haunted him—no freedom from madness.

"The bones," she said.

Lammond blinked, then nodded. "Will be burned."

"Then I am ready to go."

"Lammond," Veda began.

"I will take the very greatest of care," he assured her as he ushered Angharad out the door.

35

THOUGH THEY WERE both stoneworks, raised by the ancients for who knew what purpose, the Whistling Man wasn't the longstone in the green.

There were no heaths surrounding it, just the dark waves rolling against the shingles, the limestone cliff rising high behind it. The air was sharp with the bite of salty spray. There was no ghostsong riding the hills about it, just the wind as it breathed through the holed stone, setting up an eerie counterpoint to a music Tom heard in his mind; just the tide as it washed the shingles.

When the stone came into view, he'd sent Edrie's horse back to the inn with a slap on its rump, then made his slow way across the shingled stones of the beach. He looked for features in the grey face of the stone as he approached it, but though the moonlight was teasing, sending shadows scurrying every way he turned, it showed him only the grey exterior of rough granite.

"Elspeth," he said softly.

The wind stole her name, carried it through the hole in the stone, then away up the height of the cliff face.

Tom bent down, searching through the shingles until he found one sharp enough to draw blood. He weighed it in his hand, then took a firm grip and cut open his palm.

Left hand. Heart hand.

He laid the bloody palm against the face of the long-stone, grinding the open wound against the rough surface. Pain flared, but he put it from him, concentrating instead on what he sought.

He heard the wind, still singing through the stone's hole, but it grew distant now. The sound of the tide faded with it.

Close at hand, he heard hoofbeats on the strand. The belling of the stag as it called to the moon.

His vision dimmed, until shore and sea were washed away, until all that filled his sight was the grey stone.

And the face that gazed out at him from the granite.

Awake, not dreaming now, he had stepped across. Like called to like, blood to blood—even Summerblood as thin as was his own. The spill of crimson from his veins onto the stone had carried him away.

Into the green.

"Elspeth," he said again.

The ghostsong cried out all around them, winding from wave to wave across the rolling backs of the heathered hills. Soundlessly, her lips shaped his name.

And he remembered once again. But this time, somehow, he could bear the pain.

"You have to go," she said. "They're coming for you—I heard them talking in the village."

She had arrived out of breath—running from her father's yard outside the village to where he was mending Farmer Doak's fences in the hills.

"We'll go together."

She shook her head. "I can't."

"But—"

"I do love you. But I can't go. Not now."

He had thought—for one terrified moment he had thought that she no longer loved him. It wasn't until later that he learned why she wouldn't go: she was carrying their child.

She meant to wait until the hue and cry died down, then make her way to the coast where she would wait in her pregnancy for him to come to her. Better that, than to live like an outlaw in the hills and chance a miscarriage. She knew if she told him, he wouldn't go.

"I'll wait for you," she said. "But not here. I'll leave word with Anna."

"I . . ."

How to tell her how full his heart was for her?

"Oh, go, my heart!" she told him. "Go, before they catch you."

So he fled.

Into the hills with his witchblood, he fled. But he crept back that night to see her one more time before the wilds would swallow him for Dath knew how long.

And couldn't find her.

Not at her home, though he dared to creep into the house itself, with her family asleep around him while he searched.

Not in his nook, in Farmer Doak's barn, waiting for him.

Not anywhere in the village or around it.

When he found her, it was at the place where he'd been mending the fences, where she'd come to warn him. She lay in a pool of her own blood—the tendons severed in her legs and arms, her spine broken, the tongue cut from her mouth. Punishment for warning a witch. She would run no more. She would hold him no more. She would speak to him no more.

Miraculously, she still lived.

But the hurt he caused her when he hoisted her into his arms proved it to be no miracle. Rather a curse—like the Summerblood was a curse, for it had done this to her.

He took her to a healer in the hills—an old wise woman. She was no witch, but close enough to being one that the folk shunned her. Except when they needed her cures and potions. She was a simple herbwife, but skilled.

Though not skilled enough to help him.

"I can't give her back her voice," she told him, the anguish plain in her features. "I can't make her walk again."

Tom hadn't known despair until that day.

"But what can I do for her?"

The herbwife merely shook her head.

Tom looked at where Elspeth lay by the fire. Her eyes were open, dark with pain. Her features as white as the bandages the herbwife had used to bind her wounds.

Elspeth knew what he could do for her. She told him with her gaze.

"No," he said, shaking his head. "I can't."

You must, her gaze pleaded.

"I will care for you," he said.

But he knew as well as she what that would mean. He would have to take her far—far from where folk knew that odd Naghatty boy who could see things in the hills and talked of them in wondering tones. He would have to work to earn their keep, while she lay unattended in a bed, unable to care for herself, unable to move, unable to do anything but stare up at the ceiling of whatever home they could make for themselves.

For they weren't gentry, with the wealth to hire servants to care for her and amuse her. They were farming folk, and he wore not only the curse of witchery in his blood but the curse of poverty as well. Such a life as lay before her now promised only torment.

I could never live like that, her gaze told him.

"I don't have your courage," he told her.

Then you must find it, my heart.

So find it he did.

He bore her away from the herbwife's, away into the hills to the place she'd loved the best, where an ancient stonework stood guard on the brow of a rise and looked out across the sea of gorse.

There he laid the blade to her skin.

There he wept as the blood flowed.

There he laid her to rest under the thick sod at the foot of the stone.

There he fell into an exhausted sleep and stepped into the green, where her features regarded him from the stone.

Oh, my heart, she said. *Be not so sad. I can see into forever from this view.*

There the wind blew; the ghostsong rode the hills.

There she told him why she had bid him go while she stayed.

There she told him of the child that had died inside her when the men had hurt her so.

There his soul died inside him.

You must not blame yourself, she said. *I will endure. I will wait for you.*

There he realized that he could live no more. But he had spent all his courage on the one deed. There was none left over for what he must do now.

Live for us both, she told him. *Go gentle, my heart.*

But he could no longer hear her. He heard only the howl of the pack—the hounds of his guilt, snapping at his heels. Her lips moved, but the words he took from them were, Be a coward no more.

So he went to war, that war might accomplish what his own courage could not.

But he had survived.

A patchwork man, forever haunted. One leg lame. One eye missing. One heart broken. One soul lost to the green.

And then it was no longer a matter of courage. For if he died, he knew he must face her, and how could he face her with what he had made of his life?

Live for us both.

He had spent the promise of his life on nothing of worth.

Go gentle.

But gentleness was too long fled.

The face in the stone smiled at him as he stood now before it in the green.

I have waited so long for you, she said.

"I was never worthy of you. I was never worthy of anything."

Only you saw that—no one else. You have always been worthy in my eyes.

Tears welled up, blurring his vision.

"I . . . I will be with you soon," he said.

You have always been with me.

"I want to help her . . . the witch. Angharad . . ."

He told her of what had brought Angharad to Cathal, of Lammond and the *glascrow,* of her kindness, of her worth.

"If I help her," he said, "perhaps then it will make amends for all I've left undone."

There is no judgment in the green, she said.

Tom remembered the stag. The moon in its eyes. The wisdom and the mystery. But never judgment.

I, too, lost all hope, the stag told him, time and again. *I, too, suffered.*

Like the face in the stone, the stag spoke but never judged. That he brought on himself—with the hounds of his guilt that he set loose in the green.

What you do, Elspeth said, *you must do because it is within you to do—not to make amends.*

Tom swallowed hard. This time he would keep his courage. This time he would heed the true words that she said—not what he heard in their place.

"Tell me what I must do," he said.

36

"WHAT YOU NEED is a wizard."

Lammond shook his head. "What I need is magic—and I don't much care what kind, or who wields it for me."

They stood on the shingled beach before the Whistling Man. Lammond was dapper as always, his back straight, a gleam of anticipation heightening that odd good humor that was invariably in his eyes. Beside him, Angharad presented a disheveled appearance. Her fishergirl's garb was stained and torn from what she'd already been through this evening. Her red hair fell free, tossing about her face by the wind that came in from the dark waves and whistled through the stone. She had her journeybag over her shoulder, the comforting weight of her small harp in it.

"The green is a state of mind," she said. "And a place."

"It is power."

"Yes—but not killing power. For that you need wizardry. *Black* wizardry."

Because the *glascrow* killed only the green.

She listened to the waves wash ashore, and the whistle

of the wind as it bored through the hole in the longstone.
The shingles shifted underfoot when she stepped closer.
The moon was near to setting, but still visible in the west-
ern sky, hanging low upon the rim of the limestone cliff
that edged the strand.

"I can accept witcheries," Lammond said. "I know
they're real. But wizardry? I think not."

Angharad shook her head. "What makes the one
more believable to you than the other?"

"Witchery is merely a word for what we are all capable
of—heightened nightsight, an empathy shared with
beasts, a utilization of the more obscure abilities of our
minds. Nothing that science can't explain away. Wizardry
is spells and enchantments. Fairy tales."

"And the green?"

She could hear it sing in the doleful whistle of the
longstone. She could taste its proximity, the rich tapestry
of its otherworldly reaches, green and close at hand. Cutting across it was the trace of a familiar presence. Al-
though she recognized it, she put no name to it—neither
speaking it aloud, nor even in her mind.

"It's where we go when we die," Lammond said.
"Some sort of spirit realm, I'd think, where ghosts live.
No different from the afterworld of the Dathers—just
given another name."

"So you can believe in ghosts—but not wizardry?"

"I am . . . open-minded about ghosts."

Of course he would be, haunted as he was by the
specters of his three dead sisters. But what of the lords
he'd killed? Did they haunt him too?

"Then what of the *glascrow*?" she asked. "Isn't it a
magic talisman? Doesn't it reek of wizardry to you?"

"No."

"Broom and Heather! Why *not*?"

"Because it, too, operates on scientific principles.
The man I got it from explained it to me. It's not the

puzzle-box itself, so much as the focus a witch's mind acquires as she follows its patterns, that gives it its power.''

Why couldn't he see the contradiction in what he said? Angharad wondered. Magic wasn't real, except for the one spell he needed—it was a child's reasoning. She had anticipated more from a man of his obvious intelligence, but when she thought about it, what could she expect from one who hid such a dangerous madness behind his calm logic?

There was another contradiction as well.

''Why do you trust me to do your bidding?'' she asked. ''What makes you think I won't simply turn this magic upon you?''

Not that she could—but if he believed the *glascrow* could harm those without the Summerblood, then surely he must have considered that.

''Because I have your word that you won't.''

''When did I promise you that?''

''You will promise it to me now.''

That was easily enough done because the *glascrow* couldn't harm him.

''I promise,'' she said. ''But what's to make me keep that promise?''

Quicker than she could have believed possible, his sword was in his hand, the tip touching her throat.

''Because I will kill you if you don't. And if I'm not quick enough to do so while I live, then I'll do so after death.''

So, Angharad thought. He believes that much in ghosts.

''I . . . see,'' she said.

The tip of the sword was suddenly gone from where it touched her throat, the steel whispering back into its scabbard.

''Someone's been here,'' Lammond said in a conversational tone, as though the past few moments had never happened.

He approached the stone and indicated the smear of fresh blood on its granite surface, but Angharad had already seen it. Unlike the swordsman, however, she knew what it meant.

Blood to blood. Like calling to like.

Oh, yes. She knew.

Where have you gone? she thought. Into the green you feared so much? And why now? Why choose this night of all nights to reclaim your heritage?

"This night's too busy for my liking," Lammond said. "Everywhere we turn, there's someone abroad where they shouldn't be."

He gave Angharad a sharp look, but she merely shrugged.

"Or," Lammond went on, "not where they should be."

He had told her of Edrie's promise to wait for him with horses at the foot of the Hill in case the night's work went badly and an alarm was raised. But Edrie hadn't been there—unless, Lammond had concluded, it had been the innkeeper who had clattered by them as they stepped onto Bellsilver Lane.

Angharad had said nothing then, and said nothing now. But she had recognized the spark of Tom Naghatty's thoughts as he rode by—just as she could sense his Summerblood in the red smear that colored the holed stone.

But she kept his name hidden, else he might be drawn into the night's business, and that she would not allow. He had suffered enough.

"Never mind," Lammond said. "We've work to do."

He took the iron box from the satchel he carried it in, but Angharad shook her head.

"First the fingerbones," she said.

"The fingerbones."

He spoke as though he regretted his promise.

"It will help open the way into the green," she said.

"I'm not so sure I'm ready for ghosts," he replied, more to himself than her, but he left the bag of bones with her and went off along the shore to collect some wood.

While he was gone, Angharad took one of her rowan twigs from the bundle in her pocket. When he returned, she prepared the fire. Waking a flame in the rowan, she set it upon the wood and moments later the driftwood was burning. Sparks hissed and crackled in the flames.

"A pretty trick," Lammond said.

He reached for the bones, but Angharad shook her head.

"I must do this," she said.

Steeling herself, she opened the bag, then one by one she took the fingerbones out and dropped them into the fire. Each tiny bone she touched woke a shiver in her; she relived the pain of each witch who had died to fatten Aron Corser's purse. And as she gathered their pain . . . with each hurt she took into herself . . . she could hear a Summerborn soul fly free. Their voices were blue-gold sparks on the wind, an exultant chorus that sped away, beyond the ache of their worldly trappings . . . away and beyond . . .

By the time she was done, she already stood half on the strand, half in the green. She could hear the wind and waves, but they traveled across seas of heathered hills as well as the strand where the bone-fire burned in the shadow of the Whistling Man.

"These were another form of calling-on," she said as she took her harp from her journeybag. "In the old days. The bone-fires burned on hilltops, calling out to the Summerlord, hill to hill, wave to wave . . ."

Lammond was strangely quiet.

Sitting with the fire between herself and the holed stone, Angharad brought her harp onto her lap. She woke a chord, then a spill of harmonic notes, searching until she found the key that the wind played as it whistled through the stone. There was a flat rock that she had set by the fire and she indicated it now.

"Put it there," she said.

There was no need for her to say more. He knew what she meant.

Oh, Ballan, give me strength, she thought.

Lammond took the *glascrow* from its iron casing and set it on the stone.

Angharad stared at the puzzle-box's evil pattern.

Lord of Broom and Heather, she called, sending her thoughts out into the night. Hafarl. Arn. Tarasen. Lend me the courage I need.

She touched fingers to the strings of her harp. The small instrument sounded against the moan of the wind, against the whisper of the waves, its music far too resonant for an instrument of its size. Around her, the strand began to fade.

She was in that twilight between the worlds. Two standing stones, one holed and one not. Two seas, one of water, one of land. Two fires, the fire of bones and the one in her heart. Two darknesses, the one that spoke to her from the *glascrow*—

Come walk in shadow . . .

—And the one that was already lodged in her heart.

"What music will you play?" Lammond had asked as they fetched her harp.

"The calling-on you require," she had replied.

But it wasn't true. She played, instead, a requiem, a song to call up her own death. A music that would still the beat of her heart as soon as she had the power of the *glascrow* safely drawn into her soul.

Then the shape that housed the green death would

be only what it appeared to be: a simple puzzle-box, nothing more. For like all talismans, the *glascrow* had a soul of its own. And it had a name. A name it must give her if she were to free it from its housing. A name that would allow her to take it inside her, that would let her hold it fast until the harping she called up from her instrument's strings worked its own magic and gave her her death.

"Give me your name," she said to the voice that spoke to her from the heart of the puzzle-box.

When it spoke again, when finally it named itself to her, the calling-up took them both away.

Into the green.

37

LAMMOND CIRCLED AROUND the bone-fire, studying Angharad in its flickering light. Her gaze was fixed on the puzzle-box, her fingers pulling an eerie melody from her harp that harmonized with the sound of the wind as it blew through the hole in the Whistling Man. Feeling a little uneasy, Lammond coughed into his hand, but she never looked up, never stirred at all.

She seemed to be in a trance, but that wasn't enough to explain why the hairs were rising on the nape of his neck. He had seen trances before—wise men, far in the east, who could feign death; a herbwife as she bent over her patient, searching for invisible hurts.

But this was different. He could sense something here, within the circle cast by the light of the fire. A presence.

Presences . . .

The clacking of hooves on the shingled beach stirred him from his reverie. His hand went to his sword as he peered over Angharad to see who came. A rueful smile touched his lips as he recognized the group. Edrie Doonan and the urchin Jackin, sharing one mount. Farmer Perrin on a shaggy hill pony to their left. Corser's hoyer pacing them to the right.

He let his hand fall from his sword. What had he expected? Ghosts?

But that, he had to admit, was exactly it.

"Out for an evening ride?" he asked, calling out to them.

As they drew closer, he saw that Perrin was carrying a crossbow. There was a shaft in its groove, the bowstring cocked and ready.

"Angharad!" Edrie called, ignoring him.

So that was her name.

"She's . . . away," Lammond said.

"What have you done with her?" the innkeeper demanded.

"Nothing. She's entered into some sort of trance."

Playing her harp, while her mind flew elsewhere.

Jackin slid down from his seat behind Edrie. A moment later and the innkeeper and Perrin had dismounted as well. Edrie looked about the stone, obviously trying to pierce the darker shadows.

"Where's Tom?" she asked.

"Tom?"

"Tom Naghatty."

The name recalled a lame beggar—curled in a heap of thin limbs and tattered clothing.

"Ah. The Summerborn drunkard. Haven't seen him, I'm afraid."

"I don't see him either," Jackin said at her side. "But I can feel him." He pointed at the Whistling Man. "There. By the stone."

"So you have the true sight too, have you?" Lammond asked.

Corser's witch-finders appeared to have been better at their work than he'd supposed. Lammond himself had never sensed Summerblood in the boy.

"Get away from the girl," Perrin said.

"I think not."

"Get away or I'll . . . I'll . . ."

Lammond smiled. "Or you'll what? Cut me down where I stand?" He held his hands well away from his body. "And not a weapon in my hand. That's brave, farmer."

He was about to continue when the boy suddenly shaped the Sign of Horns in the air between them.

"Arn!" Edrie breathed. Her hand reached for the fur of the hoyer that stood at her side.

Perrin merely stood with his mouth agape.

What . . . ? Lammond thought. But then he turned and saw it, too.

The Whistling Man had begun to glow. Mist spilled from the stone, weaving a circle along the edge of the bone-fire's light, shapes moving in it. And Angharad . . . His fingers twitched to shape a warding themselves.

The witch was gone.

Vanished, both her and the damned puzzle-box. But that wasn't possible. That—

The blood drained from his features. In the mist he could see figures clearly now—thin and wiry men and women, with narrow dark-skinned faces and feral eyes. They were dressed all in grey, their dark hair braided with shells and feathers.

Kowrie.

It was impossible, he thought as he stared at them, yet here they were. And though Angharad was gone, he could still hear her harping—a distant sound, as much a part of the wind that moaned through the hole in the stone as apart from it.

As they drifted towards him, he reached for his sword. Iron would stop them. Cold iron.

But the mist swirled about him. At its touch, the leather of his belt and scabbard rotted and his sword fell to the shingled stones with a clatter. Before he could bend to retrieve it, there were faces pressed up close to his. Thin but strong hands pushing him back until he was brought up short against the stone.

"Get away . . ." he told them.

His voice died as the kowrie brought three figures forth to stand in front of him. Dath help him, but he knew those faces. Knew them all too well . . .

"How . . . ?"

"You carry them with you," one of the kowrie said.

"No, I . . . I laid them to rest."

A score of years dropped from Lammond's mind and he was just a fearful boy again. Creeping from the cupboard. Cradling his dead in his tiny arms.

He'd had no tears then, but his eyes blurred now.

"With each death, you took them further from their rightful peace," another of the kowrie said.

"I didn't . . ."

A third shook her head. "You did."

"What . . . what they did to my sisters . . ." Dath, it hurt to look at them, standing there with their wounds as fresh now as he remembered them from that night. "Who are you to judge me?"

"We don't judge," they said.

"We explain."

"They called to us."

"And we came."

An old wizened kowrie stepped from their ranks.

"You took the road you did," he said.

"What would you have me do?" Lammond cried. "Leave them unavenged?"

"But there were other roads," the old kowrie said.

"There are always others."

"Even now. There are others."

Lammond shook his head. "No. This . . . this is impossible."

"Was it so sweet, your revenge?"

"Was it worthy of their memory?"

"Their pain?"

"With each death—"

"No!" Lammond cried.

"—you took them further—"

He shook his head. No. No.

"—from their rightful peace."

No.

But he looked into the eyes of his dead kin and saw the truth there. Saw their pain. Their pity. Their sorrow.

No.

But it couldn't be denied. The red rage he carried inside him went shrieking through his mind.

No!

He lifted his head, madness wailing in his eyes. It was impossible. All of it. The stone at his back, trembling like living flesh against him. The kowrie and his dead sisters ranked before him. The wind moaning, the harp music playing . . .

No.

But then they spoke, the three dead shades. Spoke with one voice.

"Poor Lamb. What pain you have known."

No.

"We know. With each life you took, we learned again. And again . . ."

Lammond could bear no more. The red rage fired his mind until only the inferno of its madness remained. Turning his face to the sky, he howled at the darkness that lay between the stars.

38

EDRIE'S GRIP TIGHTENED on the hoyer's fur as she realized that Angharad had really and truly vanished. The sound of her harp still played, but the woman herself was gone. There one moment, the next . . .

"Jackin . . . ?"

"She went away," he said in a wondering murmur. "Into the green."

The green. Paeter had known the green. But her husband was dead and gone now. And Angharad. Where had the green taken her? Arn, was the Summerblood always to be a curse to those who carried it in their veins?

"But there's a shadow lying over her," Jackin said. "It's ever so dark."

The mists continued to spill from the holed stone, circling the fire and Lammond. Edrie thought she saw shapes moving in it, but knew that couldn't be. Then Lammond began to speak.

At first she thought he spoke to them, but as he went on, she realized he saw something more than mist swirling about him.

"What does he see?" she asked Jackin.

He had the Blood. He would know.

"Kowrie," Jackin whispered. "And the dead."

"The dead?"

Was Paeter there?

As though he read her mind, Jackin added quietly, "*His* dead. Kin he had."

"Mother of Dath," Perrin cried as Lammond backed up against the stone, shivering and fearful.

The hoyer whined at Edrie's side.

When Lammond began to howl, they all backed away. The swordsman tore at his shirt, then turned and battered his head against the stone until he sank slowly to his knees, bloodied face pressed up against the granite. His mindless shouts died to a muted sobbing.

The mists sank into the ground, then were gone. But the stone continued to glow. The harping played on. The wind moaned its counterpart melody through the hole in the stone. The air about them all was charged as though a storm was almost upon them.

Lammond had fallen silent. He was just a shadow shape now, huddled against the base of the stone.

Edrie regarded the swordsman for a long moment. Then she went to her horse and took down the provision sack and blanket that was tied behind its saddle. She carried them to the fire, where she smoothed an area of the stones and shook out the blanket.

"Give me a hand," she said to the other two as she bent over Lammond.

Jackin blinked at her. "But he—"

"Can't harm anyone now," Edrie said.

"But what he did to Angharad . . ."

"There were choices made here tonight," Edrie said, "and who knows which Angharad made or did not make on her own? She came here for something; for good or ill, I believe she found it. We know nothing of this man, except for the rumors that we've heard in town. Witchblood stirs rumors, too, and you know how many of those are true. Lammond could well have been helping her.''

"With what you said your friend Tom told you," Perrin said, "I find that unlikely."

"I'll still not leave him lying there, unattended like some hurt animal. Now will you give me a hand?"

So they helped her carry Lammond to the blanket where they stretched him out. Edrie sent the others to fetch more wood to build up the fire while she tended to the swordsman's battered face. When she had done what she could for him, and the fire was burning high once more, she sat down beside it, idly poking at the flames with a length of driftwood.

Jackin and Perrin joined her. The farmer held his crossbow on his lap, a shaft still in its groove, the weapon held so that he could easily bring it to bear on Lammond. Corser's hoyer laid down between Jackin and Edrie and stared at the holed stone, head cocked as though he listened to more than the harping, more than the wind and the tide.

"What do we do now?" Perrin asked.

Edrie turned to Jackin.

"Nothing we can do," the urchin said. "Nothing but watch and wait."

Perrin looked at the holed stone, at the bone-fire which Angharad had been sitting beside when she vanished, swallowed by magic. Only her harping remained, still sounding against the murmur of wind and tide.

"But Angharad . . . ?" he began.

"What happens now," Jackin said, "happens in the green."

39

WHEN THE *GLASCROW* told Angharad its name, they were already in the green. She could feel the other-world shudder at the sound of it. There was a tremor in the ground that made her shiver where she sat. The reaches of the green grew tense and rigid. For one moment all was still, except for her harping. When the ghostsong of the wind began again, its sound was more mournful than ever.

A shadow grew from the puzzle-box, a thick tendril of blackness that coiled above it like smoke. Beyond it she could see a standing stone with a face in its granite, stone eyes watching her. Angharad thought of another ancient stonework, of a simple-minded man named Pog who had been taken into the green by the kowrie in just such a shape.

On one side of the stone stood a red-flanked stag. On the other stood Tom Naghatty.

What are you doing here? she wanted to ask him, but she knew she had no time for questions. She had to speak the *glascrow*'s name and draw it inside her; she had to bind it to herself so that when her death came, it would die with her.

But Tom spoke its name first.

She shivered at the sound of it, felt the borders of the green draw more taut. She called the name herself before the echo of Tom's voice had a chance to fade; she called it quickly, desperately, but the soul of the *glascrow* could only heed one master at a time.

With sick dread she watched the black smoke disengage itself from the puzzle-box and fly to where Tom stood. He opened his mouth wide and it sped down his throat. Darkness flowed under his skin. His stance altered as his lame leg straightened. His blind eye grew hale, and shadows lived in his gaze now.

"Give it to me," she said.

"Too . . . late . . ." he replied.

"No."

"Give me . . . your song."

He meant give him her death.

"I can't," she said.

Not that she couldn't, but that she wouldn't. This had been hers to do. She was already tainted by the *glascrow's* touch. Even if it died here, she would still carry a shadow of it inside her—though that shadow was just an echo of what Tom bore himself. She realized then that he had taken the choice from her.

"Why did you do it?" she asked.

His features continued to darken. She could feel the *glascrow's* power growing as it explored the resonances of his Summerblood. Soon it would own him completely. Soon it would spread out from his body to feed on the green.

"For your goodness," he said. "For your kindness."

Angharad could have wept.

The choice was his, the face in the stone told her.

There was an infinite sadness in its voice. Looking at the grey features, Angharad realized that she looked upon Tom's lost love. Her gaze went to Tom, slid away from his changing features and settled on the stag.

Allow him his moment of courage, the stag said.

"Quickly now," Tom said. "Before . . ."

Before it was too late.

"I . . . can't . . ." Angharad began, but her fingers were already pulling the final chord from her harp's strings.

The wind died. The ghostsong fell silent. The land ceased to breathe. A look of extraordinary peace crossed Tom's features, then he closed his eyes. He sank to his knees, smiling, and pitched over on his side.

In her mind, Angharad could hear the frustrated howl of the *glascrow* as it died with him.

Then silence.

For a very long time, only silence.

Finally the wind began to murmur once more. First one soft breath, then another, until it was traveling over the land, hill to hill, heathered wave to heathered wave. The ghostsong chorused behind it.

Angharad saw a pack of dogs encircling them—dark feral hounds that seemed to melt into the ground like frost before the morning sun. She looked at the stone, but the features in its granite surface were gone. The puzzle-box lay in front of her, empty and harmless. Its inlaid pattern of ebon and silver was innocent now—except for how it reminded her of the shadow she carried inside her.

But we all carry shadows, don't we? she thought.

Hugging her harp to her chest with one hand, she rose and knelt by Tom's side. Her gaze was thick with tears. She took his head onto her lap and softly stroked his brow. As the green began to fade around her, she turned her gaze to the stag, one hand still upon Tom's cooling skin.

"Pog?" she asked.

There was a sad smile in the stag's eyes.

Did you think there was but the stag in all the green? it asked her.

Angharad shook her head. "Where . . . where did he go?"

Beyond.

She could hear the whistling of the holed stone now, the murmur of the tide. The green was fading quickly.

"Is he . . . will he be well . . . ?" she asked.

But there was no reply. The green was gone and she was back on the strand with the Grey Sea lapping the shingles, the holed stone whistling above her.

She saw the fire, burning bright. Edrie and Jackin scrambling to their feet. Farmer Perrin and Magger. And Lammond—lying on a blanket, still as death, his eyes opening as though her return had called him back from some haunted place. His face was terribly bruised.

"What . . . happened?" she asked.

Her hand stilled on Tom's brow.

Lammond sat up, every movement an obvious effort as he fought some inner pain. Looking at the faces of the others, Angharad understood that they had never touched him. He had done this to himself.

His madness had done it to him.

"Did you keep your promise?" he asked.

Still, from that bruised face, in the midst of his pain, his voice was mild again, as though they were old friends, carrying on a quiet conversation.

"I didn't turn the magic upon you," she replied.

She knew that wasn't the promise he meant. But she had made him no other.

He nodded slowly. "I see."

Edrie and the others stood listening, shifting their feet on the shingles, uncertain as to what they should do.

"So it wasn't you that . . . called up the kowrie?" Lammond asked. "Called them up with their lies and illusions?"

Angharad blinked. She looked to Edrie, who shook her head, looked to Jackin.

"They showed him his dead kin," Jackin said softly. "Told him that with every gentry's life he took, he caused them further hurt. Kept them from peace. He . . . he went mad . . ."

The urchin took a few steps back as he spoke, glancing nervously at Lammond.

The swordsman nodded. "Oh, yes," he said. "I went mad. But I've learned to live with madness. It comes and goes, comes and goes . . ."

He pushed himself to his feet, swaying where he stood. With a great effort he straightened his back, smoothed down his bloodied shirt.

"It's lies I can't live with," he said. "It's knowing all those gentry will live on, while my sisters lie dead. Plain and simply dead. They're *not* ghosts, still suffering"—he gave Jackin a grim look—"but dead and long buried. Butchered by gentry"—his gaze returned to Angharad—"that you have saved."

Angharad shook her head. "The *glascrow* could never do what you wanted it to."

"Are you deaf?" Lammond asked her, the tone of his voice still mild. "I said I can't live with lies."

They were lulled, all of them, by his obvious weakness. A man who could barely stand on his own, how could he move so quickly? But move he did, as though he'd never suffered a hurt. He snatched up his sword and brought the edge of its blade whistling down at Angharad—

They were caught off guard. Perrin, too slow in bringing up his crossbow. Jackin, standing too far away. Edrie, simply stunned. The hoyer lunging, but the distance between himself and the swordsman was too great.

But Angharad moved. Her hand dove into her pocket

and came out again to fling a handful of blazing rowan twigs straight into Lammond's face. Fired by madness or not, he still stepped back as the burning twigs sprayed about him. Still stayed his blow, if only for a moment.

But that moment was enough for Magger to launch himself at Lammond's swordhand. For Perrin's crossbow shaft to find the swordsman's heart. As Lammond keeled over, the hoyer loosed his grip. The swordsman sprawled onto the stones and lay still. No one moved. They stood as motionless as the longstone, staring at the corpse. Magger stepped forward and sniffed Lammond's face, one broad paw on his chest, turning away only when he was satisfied that the man was dead.

And then there was stillness again.

The wind spoke through the hole in the stone. The tide murmured. But those left alive uttered not a word, moved not at all. Until Angharad looked away from Lammond's corpse, looked down into Tom's dead features. Her hand stroked his brow, where the skin was so cold now.

"Go gentle," she said.

And go he did, his body fading from where she held it. Tom Naghatty went away.

With the stag.

With the moon and her wisdom.

And her mystery.

Into the green.

40

THERE WAS ONLY Veda at the funeral, Veda and the men she had hired to bury Lammond. She stood in the graveyard, long after the men had finished their work and gone. She wore a black cloak, with the hood pulled over her head. Her gaze was fixed, not on the mound of fresh earth at her feet, but on the reaches of the Grey Sea that spread away from the headland where the graveyard stood.

She didn't turn as Angharad approached. Angharad wore her tinker garb again. She carried a white staff in one hand, a journeybag over one shoulder, a harp over the other. Magger padded at her side.

"I never meant him any ill," she said.

Veda nodded. "I know. He brought it on himself. I would have stopped him, but he would only have sent me away. I loved him—so how could I leave him?"

"What will you do now?" Angharad asked.

Veda shook her head. "I don't know. All I had was Lammond . . ."

Her gaze remained fixed upon the distance, to some place across the Grey Sea. Perhaps she looked to a better time, Angharad thought, to when she and Lammond had met—when he had been simply charming; before she understood the darkness he carried inside him.

"What will you do?" Veda asked.

"I have friends in Cermyn," Angharad said. "They live by Avalarn Wood. I thought I might visit with them . . ."

They stood awhile in silence, until Angharad reached out and touched the woman's shoulder.

"Come with me," she said.

Veda turned to look at her. "Travel with a tinker? To laugh."

But there were tears in her eyes.

"You've seen yourself how old pains cause new hurts," Angharad said. "Allow yourself time to heal."

"What would you know of old hurts?"

Angharad thought of those she had loved and lost. Her husband. Her clan. Friends.

Something in Angharad's features made Veda slowly nod her head. She looked away again, out over the sea.

"I have only the one skill," she said.

"You can always learn another."

Veda turned to look at her again. "Why would you want to help me?"

Angharad leaned on her staff. One hand reached down to ruffle Magger's fur.

"Because I was helped once. I didn't want it. I fought it. But in the end, it made me whole again. What I lost, I still miss. Desperately, sometimes. But I can bear it now."

"I don't know if I have your courage."

"I will lend you some, then," Angharad said. "Until you find your own."

Still Veda hesitated.

"Come," Angharad said.

Taking her arm, she led Veda away. Together they walked through the graveyard, arm in arm, Magger at Angharad's side. Remembering how Lammond had been able to see the kowrie, without Hafarl's gift in his blood, she wondered if witcheries could be taught as well as born to. Hadn't Lammond said—

Witchery is merely a word for what we are all capable of . . .

Though he had been so very wrong about so very much, *that* at least had the ring of truth about it.

She glanced at her companion. Perhaps the green could help Veda, as it had helped her.

It was worth a try. Not just for Veda's sake, but for all the housey-folk, blind to the green. If one could be taught to see, then might they not all be able to in time? With the differences lessened between Summerborn and those without the gift, would there not be that much less reason for one to cause the other pain?

Surely it was worth the attempt.

She thought she heard the distant belling of a stag, but as she paused to listen more closely for it, Magger bumped his head against her hand. She gave the hoyer a quick pat, then the three of them walked on.

Appendix: Tunes from the Kingdoms of the Green Isles

The following tunes for small harp and other melody instruments are from the repertoire of the tinker Angharad. All tunes are copyright © 1993 by Charles de Lint; all rights reserved.

CAYA'S SLIP JIG

FLIGHT OF THE HERON

FLOODROAD

GEESE ON THE WING

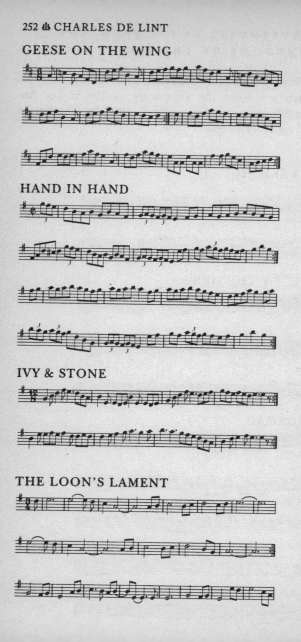

HAND IN HAND

IVY & STONE

THE LOON'S LAMENT

THE LOON'S LAMENT (CONTINUED)

MICHAEL COPELAND'S REEL

PIPER'S DRAM

THE OLD RED CAT

TEN YEARS TODAY

THE WATER RAT

WESTLIN WIND

[ALL TUNES WRITTEN AND TRANSCRIBED BY CHARLES DE LINT, EXCEPT FOR ''THE LOON'S LAMENT,'' WHICH WAS WRITTEN BY CHARLES DE LINT AND TRANSCRIBED BY JOHN WOOD. THANKS, JOHN.]

FANTASY BESTSELLERS
FROM TOR

☐ 52261-3 BORDERLANDS $4.99
        edited by Terri Windling & Lark Alan Arnold   Canada $5.99

☐ 50943-9 THE DRAGON KNIGHT $5.99
        Gordon R. Dickson   Canada $6.99

☐ 51371-1 THE DRAGON REBORN $5.99
        Robert Jordan   Canada $6.99

☐ 52003-3 ELSEWHERE $3.99
        Will Shetterly   Canada $4.99

☐ 55409-4 THE GRAIL OF HEARTS $4.99
        Susan Schwartz   Canada $5.99

☐ 52114-5 JINX HIGH $4.99
        Mercedes Lackey   Canada $5.99

☐ 50896-3 MAIRELON THE MAGICIAN $3.99
        Patricia C. Wrede   Canada $4.99

☐ 50689-8 THE PHOENIX GUARDS $4.99
        Steven Brust   Canada $5.99

☐ 51373-8 THE SHADOW RISING $5.99
        Robert Jordan (Coming in October '93)   Canada $6.99

Buy them at your local bookstore or use this handy coupon:
Clip and mail this page with your order.

Publishers Book and Audio Mailing Service
P.O. Box 120159, Staten Island, NY 10312-0004

Please send me the book(s) I have checked above. I am enclosing $ _____
(Please add $1.25 for the first book, and $.25 for each additional book to cover postage and handling.
Send check or money order only—no CODs.)

Name _____

Address _____

City _____ State/Zip _____

Please allow six weeks for delivery. Prices subject to change without notice.

MORE BESTSELLING
FANTASY FROM TOR

☐	50392-9	**DRAGON SEASON** *Michael Cassutt*	$4.99 Canada $5.99
☐	51716-4	**THE FOREVER KING** *Warren Murphy and Ellen Kushner*	$5.99 Canada $6.99
☐	50360-0	**GRYPHON'S EYRIE** *Andre Norton & A.C. Crispin*	$3.95 Canada $4.95
☐	52248-6	**THE LITTLE COUNTRY** *Charles de Lint*	$5.99 Canada $6.99
☐	50518-2	**THE MAGIC OF RECLUCE** *L.E. Modesitt, Jr.*	$4.99 Canada $5.99
☐	50249-3	**SISTER LIGHT, SISTER DARK** *Jane Yolen*	$3.95 Canada $4.95
☐	55815-4	**SOLDIER OF THE MIST** *Gene Wolfe*	$3.95 Canada $4.95
☐	51112-3	**STREET MAGIC** *Michael Reaves*	$3.99 Canada $4.99
☐	51445-9	**THOMAS THE RHYMER** *Ellen Kushner*	$3.99 Canada $4.99

Buy them at your local bookstore or use this handy coupon:
Clip and mail this page with your order.

Publishers Book and Audio Mailing Service
P.O. Box 120159, Staten Island, NY 10312-0004

Please send me the book(s) I have checked above. I am enclosing $ _____
(Please add $1.25 for the first book, and $.25 for each additional book to cover postage and handling.
Send check or money order only—no CODs.)

Name _____

Address _____

City _____ State/Zip _____

Please allow six weeks for delivery. Prices subject to change without notice.